ONE SHOT

ONE SHOT

JONATHAN FLY

Jonathan Fly
ONE SHOT

Cover design: Miblart

Published by Spines
ISBN: 979-8-89569-706-1

Dedicated to the dreamers.

ACKNOWLEDGMENTS

Thank you to the wonderful people of Anthony, Kansas; Pleasanton, Kansas; Fort Scott, Kansas; and St. Joseph, Missouri.

Heartfelt thanks to my Beta readers, my family, friends, and everyone who has supported this labor of love.

CONTENTS

CHAPTER 1

August 21, 1982.

The loud noise of breaking glass, loud thuds, and screaming voices startled twelve-year-old Josh Bailey from a peaceful slumber. The book he had been reading when he fell asleep was resting on his chest. He glanced at his alarm clock and noticed it said 2:15 a.m.

"Get the fuck out.", he heard his mother, Angel scream. "I told you to never hit me again."

" I'm not going anywhere." The assailant yelled back at her. He placed his hand over Angel's face and shoved her backward into the brown paneling of the living room. He punched her hard in her mouth and blood began to ooze from her lip and she fell to the floor, screaming.

"You son-of-a-bitch." She yelled.

The abuser kicked her hard in the ribs several times then he pulled out the .45 pistol that he kept hidden between his faded jeans and his back. He grabbed the barrel of the weapon and hit her hard on her head with the butt of the gun twice, rendering her speechless. Pistol whipped.

Josh heard the crack of the gun on his mom's head, but he didn't see it. He knew it was bad when his mom's shouting suddenly stopped. He quickly arose from his bed and slipped his feet into his sneakers without tying them, grabbed his 30-ounce aluminum baseball bat, and made his way down the narrow hallway of their mobile home quietly yet quickly. When he reached the living room, he saw a man standing over his mother who was lying on the floor nearly unconscious with blood streaming down her face. She was barely breathing. The man reeked of alcohol and cigarettes. The man did not see it coming when Josh swung the bat and connected directly with the attacker's right hand which still had the gun in it breaking the man's knuckles. The ping of the bat against his hand forced the man to immediately drop his weapon. The big man had no time to react. Without hesitation, Josh took another swing, this time connecting with the man's shin, splintering the bone. The assailant went down to the floor grasping at his now broken shin and screaming in pain, his eyes closed from the agony he was suffering. That unwise reflexive action gave Josh an open shot in the man's face. Josh reared back and as hard as he could, took another swing, this time the bat landed between the man's upper lip and nose knocking out a few of the man's teeth and sending them into his throat. Blood spewed from his mouth and nose, the force of the bat knocked him backward and he hit the back of his head on the wooden coffee table.

Josh dropped his bat and knelt next to his mom. "Mom?" he said. "Mom?' He shouted louder. She wouldn't answer. He glanced over at the man who was mumbling something. Blood was oozing from his mouth and nose. Wincing in pain.

"You son-of-a-bitch.", Josh yelled out. He noticed the gun lying on the floor. With his adrenaline pumping, he crawled to the weapon and picked it up shakily with his right hand. It felt heavy in his thin hand and skinny arm. He had seen enough movies and television shows to know that the hammer needed to be cocked back. Josh was seated on the floor struggling to get the gun cocked. When he finally succeeded, he aimed the heavy gun at the man's head. The man saw him and tried to move but his shattered shin prevented him from standing or crawling. He was trapped between the coffee table and the gun pointed at his head.

The evil man said, "I'm your fa…" but would never finish the sentence. Josh squeezed the trigger propelling the bullet through the man's right eye and out the back of the assailant's head. Gray matter, blood, and pieces of skull exited the man's skull and sprayed the couch and coffee table behind him. The man's head rested on the coffee table. His eyes were closed, and his blood-filled mouth was open. There was a gurgling sound coming from the man's mouth. The kick from the gun sent Josh's hand back into his face, hitting him in the nose. His nose began to bleed. His skinny body fell backward, and he banged his head against the wall. His ears rang from the loud shot of the pistol.

Josh dropped the gun and crawled to his mother. She was lying awkwardly on the floor, her head tilted grotesquely and resting against the wood-paneled wall. Bruised and badly beaten with blood streaming down her beautiful face. She had two large gashes on her head that had blood coming out of them, staining her light brown hair.

Josh grabbed her shoulders and tried again to make her speak. "Mom, wake up" he yelled. "MOOOM."

Angel opened one of her eyes as far as she could and mumbled something to Josh. He couldn't understand what she was saying. He leaned in and put his ear close to his mother's mouth. She whispered. "He's...your...," and closed her only open eye.

"What?" Josh shouted.

No response. Josh shook her again, "MOOOOOM", he shouted but she could not speak. Her breathing was labored and short. He grabbed her and held her close to his chest. Then he laid her down gently onto the blood-soaked shag carpet and watched helplessly as his beautiful mother exhaled for the last time.

Out of breath and unsure what to do, Josh mindlessly looked around the room. Shattered glass was everywhere. Broken picture frames were scattered about. Josh reached down and flicked away the broken glass from one of the photos with his fingers. It was the last photograph of him and his mother that had been taken of them together last Christmas. He grabbed the 5X7 picture that was in the frame, folded it into quarters, and went back to his room. There, he put on clean shorts and placed the folded photograph in his pocket, put on a T-shirt, and made his way back to the living room. He glanced over and noticed the necklace that was resting on his mother's neck. Josh had given the necklace to his mother for her birthday a few months ago. He gingerly released the clasp on the back of the necklace and placed it in his pocket with the photograph.

By the time he got outside and sat down on the steps that led to the small, front porch in front of their home he heard sirens in the distance. He waited silently.

* * *

Joshua Bailey was born on April 2nd, 1970. He never knew his father. His mother, Angel, told him when he was little that his father had left just before he was born, and Angel had no idea where he was. Josh was a skinny kid with blue eyes, and messy, short, brown hair. He was the smallest kid in his class. He hated school because he was constantly being picked on and made fun of. The bullies at school teased him about his cheap clothes and called him and his mother 'white trash.'

He had no friends, so he spent most of his time reading. It was his escape into other places and meeting other people. He sat alone at lunch and when there were games and two captains would choose players for their team, Josh was always the last one. He was never chosen; he was simply the only kid left. He rarely spoke to anyone except for his mom.

CHAPTER 2

The small town of Pleasanton, Kansas, sat unnoticeable along US 69 in eastern Kansas. It was a farming community forty-five minutes south of Kansas City. It had a Casey's convenience store and a Dollar General store. A couple of small cafes and one lonely bar. It was a tight-knit community where everyone knew everyone else. The Sherriff's department was comprised of just the sheriff and one deputy. The nearest hospital was in Garnett, Kansas, thirty-eight miles west of Pleasanton. While Pleasanton had a clinic, the lack of an emergency room made it difficult and slow for residents to receive urgently needed help. Neither of which would be needed tonight.

It was a warm and seemingly airless August night at the Blue View Mobile Home Park outside of town. The origin of the name and the person who came up with it remained unknown. There was nothing blue about it and there certainly was no view. The fifteen mobile homes resting there were lined at an angle to the street, which was a U-shaped drive called 'Blue Drive'. It was a peaceful place. During spring and summer, Josh would mow some of the lawns for the residents there for $5 per yard. Nothing exciting ever happened there. Most folks would spend their evenings inside their homes watching television and going to bed at a reasonable hour. On this night, however, the fight at the Bailey home awakened the residents of the Blue View Mobile Home Park. No neighbors ventured out until assured of safety and cessation of violence.

When deputy John Hilts arrived at Lot 6, he found Josh sitting quietly on the front steps of the small porch that led to the door of the trailer. Deputy Hilts pulled up to Josh's lot with red and blue lights flashing. Josh had to shield his eyes from the bright headlights of the police cruiser. Hilts noticed Josh shielding his eyes and dimmed the headlights but left the red and blue beacons on. He got out of the car and walked toward Josh. Joshua's nose still had blood trickling down to his mouth. Deputy Hilts was a tall and skinny young man. He had a mustache and was dressed smartly in his uniform. His pistol in its holster on his right side

"Josh, are you okay?" Hilts asked. "Are you alright? What happened?"

Without a word, Josh tilted his head back, indicating the trailer's front door.

Deputy Hilts asked, "Is anyone in there armed?"

Josh said quietly, "Not anymore."

Hilts slowly opened the door to the trailer and what he saw when he went inside shocked him. He had only been a deputy for a year and being only 25 years old, he had never experienced a violent crime scene, let alone one this horrible. Nothing could have prepared him for what he saw. The living room was filled with glass shards and framed photographs scattered across the ugly, brown, carpeted floor. The kitchen was in complete disarray. The sink was full of unwashed dishes and the trash can was overflowing. It reeked of nasty garbage. In the living room, he saw blood splatter on the couch and coffee table. The two bodies lying on the floor motionless. The male's head was laid back on the coffee table with his mouth gaping open. Hilts immediately noticed the bullet hole in the man's right eye and the blood and pieces of skull splattered on the couch behind him. He did not recognize him. The female, Angel, was lying on the carpet a few feet away. Blood covered most of her face. Hilts choked for a second and he realized the woman was Angel Bailey. He had been here before a few times for domestic disturbances but none of those times compared to what he was seeing now. He knew they were both dead, but he checked each of them for a pulse anyway. He could not find one on either body. He noticed the bat and the gun both lying on the floor, and he saw one spent shell casing. He walked carefully toward the back of the mobile home. Glancing in the bathroom and bedrooms. He made his way back outside, being careful not to disturb any evidence or step into any pools of blood. When he got outside, he saw that Josh hadn't moved from the steps.

He took a deep breath and asked, "Did you see what happened?", Hilts asked.

Josh nodded his head.

The deputy said, "I need to contact my boss and request an ambulance. Will you be okay here?"

Josh nodded again and Hilts returned to his cruiser. Josh couldn't hear what he was saying, but he could see the deputy talking on his radio. Some of Josh's neighbors began to emerge from their homes to observe what was happening. They all knew it was bad when they saw Josh sitting alone on his steps without his mother at this late hour and they could not hear her voice. A couple of them shook their heads in disbelief, one lady was crying.

Deputy Hilts got out of his cruiser and approached Josh.

He said, "Can you tell me what happened?"

Josh replied matter-of-factly, "He beat my mom and killed her, so I shot him." There was no remorse in his voice. He did what he had to do. "What happens now?" Josh asked.

Hilts took a deep breath and said, "I've contacted our Chaplain. He'll arrive shortly, and then we can proceed. For now, I need to move you away from here and put you in my car."

"Am I going to jail?" Josh inquired.

"No" Hilts replied. "I just want you to be safe and wait for the Chaplain."

The deputy escorted Josh to the cruiser and placed him in the back seat...alone.

Josh watched as deputy Holts began interviewing some of the neighbors. He could see them pointing toward Josh's trailer and talking to the deputy.

* * *

Pastor Raymond Stevens arrived a while later and exited his white Toyota Camry. He was tall, slender, and dressed in jeans and a button-down brown shirt. His hair was mostly black but had a few whisps of gray in it. He walked quickly toward Officer Hilts. They spoke to each other for a few minutes and then Officer Hilts escorted the Pastor to his cruiser where Josh sat waiting. He opened the door and said, "Josh, this is Pastor Stevens. He's going to look after you for a little while. Tomorrow, he'll take you to the sheriff's office and we'll talk some more. For now, I need you to go with him. He'll make sure you have food and a roof over your head. You may want to get some clothes from your room."

Josh shook his head, "I'm not going back in there.", he said

Josh got out of the cruiser and walked with Pastor Stevens to his waiting Camry. They got in and drove off toward the Pastor's home.

"Deputy Hilts told me what happened," Raymond said. "I'm so sorry for your loss."

Josh sat quietly. So many thoughts were going through his mind.

After a few moments, Josh asked, "What's going to happen to me?"

"Well, for now, you'll stay with my wife and me." Pastor Stevens replied. "We'll get things sorted out in the morning. Are you hungry? Do you need anything?"

"I just want my mom back," Josh said.

* * *

Only a few hours later, Josh, Pastor Stevens, and his wife, Marie were having breakfast. Josh would only take a few bites of the cereal in his bowl. He hadn't slept at all, and he was still in the same clothes he had on a few hours ago when Pastor Stevens picked him up at his trailer. The Pastor's wife, Marie said, "When you get done at the Sherriff's office, we'll go downtown and get you some more clothes."

Josh sat silently staring into the bowl of now soggy cereal.

* * *

Josh and Pastor Stevens drove to the Sheriff's office in the center of town. Exhausted, scared, and eager, he awaited his uncertain future. Neither of them spoke until they pulled into a parking spot in front of the building.

Pastor Stevens attempted to comfort Josh by guaranteeing him a place to stay, alleviating one worry from his mind. Josh nodded as if to say, 'OKAY'.

The Linn County Sheriff's office was tiny with plain, lime-green walls. As they walked in, Josh noticed a lady sitting at the front desk talking on the phone. The name plate in front of her said 'Phyllis Smith'. She was heavy-set but not unattractive. She glanced up at Josh and gave him a sad look and nodded gently at him. She hung up the phone and said, "I saw you pull up and I just let Sherriff Jackson know you're here. He'll be right out".

Pastor Stevens thanked her, and he and Josh found seats on a small bench near the lady's desk.

Less than a minute later, Sherriff Jackson appeared. Dressed perfectly in his uniform, he was a large, black man with a clean-shaven face. He had an excellent reputation among the law-abiding folks in Linn County. He shook Pastor Stevens's hand and said, "Come on back."

Leading them down a short hallway, he took them to a small room with ugly green walls that contained a table and chairs. Deputy Hilts was sitting in one of the metal chairs. He looked exhausted. It had been a long night of collecting evidence at the Bailey home.

"First, ", Chief Jackson said flatly, "I'm sorry about your mother, Josh"

Josh, who had spent the past 5 hours mostly silent, finally spoke. "If you guys would have done your job, my mom would still be alive!" he yelled. "How many times did you or Hilts come out to our house and break up a fight? How many times did you arrest these jerks only to let them out the next day? Don't tell me how sorry you are when you let this happen. You did NOTHING to stop this."

Josh's anger and disdain toward Sherriff Jackson were justified, he thought. He didn't care if what he said got him into trouble. He didn't care if they locked him in jail. He had had enough. All he wanted was his mom back. He felt like crying, but he fought the urge. He wasn't about to let these people see him cry.

"I know it's hard for you to understand, Josh," Chief Jackson said. "Our hands are tied. Those guys were repeatedly released by the judge due to your mother's decision not to press charges."

Josh said, "It shouldn't be her responsibility to press charges. You know those assholes would threaten her if she did."

They sat in silence for a moment until Chief Jackson spoke at last, "Deputy Hilts informed me of your statement, but we need some more details. Tell me what happened."

Josh told him about the fight and how the man had beaten his mom and he was pretty sure that the guy pistol-whipped her and that he used his bat to beat the man. He told them about the gun and that he shot him in the head. "I'd do again if I had to.", He spoke. He wanted to ask the man's name but decided to wait.

Chief Jackson said, "That seems to fit with the evidence that we collected. We're waiting for the ballistics report to come back to confirm a couple of things, and then we'll talk to the prosecutor. She'll decide what to do at that point. I don't foresee her pressing charges against you considering the circumstances."

"I don't give a rat's ass what she does,", Josh said. "Where's my mom?"

Chief Jackson replied, "She's at the morgue right now. The medical examiner has tests to run to discover the exact cause of death. That will take a few days."

"I know how she died," Josh said, "She was beaten to death by an asshole that should have been locked up a long time ago." Josh shook his head in disbelief. He said, "Who was he? What's his name?"

Chief Jackson said, "His name is Bruce Williams. He was released from Lansing prison two days ago."

Josh asked, "What was he in there for?"

Chief Jackson did not want to answer that question, so he hesitated and finally said, "Attempted murder and assault. He was there for eight years."

Josh screamed and said, "And you idiots let him out? What is wrong with you people?" Josh was steaming. "The courts let him out so he could come here and beat my mother to death." He exclaimed.

Chief Jackson sighed and looked at Josh warily. He understood Josh's anger and frustration and he felt genuine sympathy for him. The Chief looked at Pastor Stevens who had spent the entire time in silence. Then he asked Josh if he had any other family members they could call. Josh shook his head, "No. It's just me and my mom." He spoke.

Pastor Stevens said, "He's welcome to stay with us for as long as he needs to or until this all gets sorted out. We'll get him some clothes, make sure he's well-fed, and provide a safe place for him"

Chief Jackson nodded and said, "Okay. Josh, you're free to go. You're not under arrest and we're not going to place you into a foster home just yet. Stay with Pastor Stevens and he and his wife will look out for you. Either myself or the prosecutor will be in touch soon."

Josh sat motionless.

"Again, we're sorry for your loss." Sheriff Jackson said.

"Screw you." Was all Josh could think of to say as he walked out of the room.

CHAPTER 3

The obituary read:

Angel Katherine Bailey, 32 of Pleasanton,
Passed away on August 21, 1982
She was born on June 5th, 1950
She is survived by her son Joshua Bailey
Services will be held at Smith Brother's mortuary on Friday,
August 26th at 1:00 p.m.
Graveside service will be held at Pleasanton Cemetery
immediately following the funeral.

That was all it said. Pastor Stevens wrote it and paid for it to be published in newspapers all over Kansas hoping maybe a relative of Josh would happen upon it and contact someone in Pleasanton. He wished he had more information, like Angel's parents or any other next of kin. Josh could only tell him about a couple of his mom's friends in Pleasanton and when he contacted them, they were of no help. Angel had never told anyone in Pleasanton about her past or where she had lived before moving there when she was 17. All he could do was hope and pray that a relative of Angel's would turn up.

In Pleasanton, there is a group of citizens who would help those in need either with food housing, or clothing for people who needed it. Using their limited funds, the group chose to pay for Angel Bailey's funeral, opting for an affordable coffin and a small headstone.

The funeral for Angel Bailey was a somber event. The funeral home smelled of fresh flowers. Sad organ music played softly through speakers scattered throughout the building. The room that the funeral was held in was small with only a few rows of seats for the bereaved to sit in. At the front of the room was Angel's closed coffin. The funeral director mentioned to Pastor Stevens that the damage done to Angel's body was too severe and thought it best for people to not see her. There were only a few bouquets of flowers in front of Angel's coffin that had been sent by friends of Angel's. Josh sat alone in the front row with Pastor Stevens and his wife, Marie sitting directly behind him while a couple of friends of Angel's said a few words. Then Pastor Stevens went to the podium and made a brief eulogy. Josh wasn't paying attention to him. He sat motionless with his head down.

It was a hot, sunny day with only a few clouds in the sky. There were not many people in attendance. The funeral procession going to the cemetery had only a few cars following the hearse that carried Angel Bailey to her final resting place. One of those was Pastor Stevens' Camry which held Josh in the back seat. Josh decided a few days before that he didn't want to ride in the limo, so it wasn't needed. At the grave site, there was a green tent that covered the site. Sadly, there was only one chair placed there and it was for Josh to sit in. Pastor Stevens recited a few scriptures from the Bible and said some kind words. When the graveside service ended, a woman Josh didn't know expressed her condolences to Josh and said nice things about his mom.

"She was a wonderful woman,", she said. "If you need anything, let us know" Then she said, "She's in a better place now." This enraged Josh as he believed the perfect place for her was alive and with him.

She stated, "This was God's will."

Josh turned and glared at her. Without another word, she departed in her car along with the other "well-wishers".

When everyone had gone, except for Pastor Stevens and his wife, who waited patiently by their Camry, Josh sat still in the velvet-covered chair alongside his mother's grave. Alone, at that moment, he finally shed a tear. He knew he would never see his mom again.

The funeral for Bruce Williams was held the next day. There was no one in attendance.

* * *

The Wichita Eagle was perhaps the largest newspaper in the entire state of Kansas. It had subscribers all over central and southern Kansas. The paper was delivered either by mail or courier to homes daily.

Woodrow 'Woody' Bailey and his wife, Loanne of

Anthony, Kansas, were one of those subscribers. They had just returned home from a day in the fields when Loanne and Woody were sitting in their respective chairs at their farm and skimming the mail, newspapers, etc. Loanne saw it first and let out an audible gasp.

Woody looked at her and asked, "What's wrong?"

She quickly handed the Eagle to him and said, "Could this be her?" and pointed to the obituary for Angel Katherine Bailey.

Woody's eyes widened as he read the obituary.

He said out loud, "Oh my god!"

Loanne said, "We need to find out if it's her, and if it is, we have to go."

"It has to be." Woody said, "Look at the birthdate and that's her full name."

Loanne said, "But it says she had a son. I didn't know she had a son."

Woody responded, "We haven't heard a thing about her in 14 years, so it's possible she had a son without us knowing."

"When does it say she died?", Woody asked, while rummaging through paperwork trying to find his family history and anything else they might need.

"August 21st" Loanne responded. "Her funeral was last Friday".

"Shit." Woody said, "We missed her funeral. Damn it."

Loanne said, "I'll find out what the phone number for the newspaper in Pleasanton is and call them to see if I can get any more information. We have to know if it's her and what happened."

Loanne found the phone number for the Linn County

Journal and hurriedly called. After speaking to a receptionist, the receptionist directed her to an editor. She didn't catch his name, she just wanted information regarding the obituary for Angel. She explained that she and Woody had just noticed Angel's obituary and were likely family and wanted any details they could provide. The voice on the other end stated that, according to the police report, someone had killed Angel during an argument at her home. The local Sherriff's office believed that her son Joshua, 12, shot and killed the man responsible for Angel's death but that hadn't been made public due to Josh's young age.

Loanne thanked him and quietly placed the phone back in its cradle. With a grim look on her face, she looked at Woody and shared the words of the newspaper editor. Woody said, "We have to go. Right now."

The call from the prosecutor's office came around 11:00 a.m. on August 29th. She informed Pastor Stevens that there would not be charges filed against Josh. The gun, bearing Bruce William's fingerprints on the barrel, was used to assault Angel, and there were no additional prints on the barrel. She went on to say that the autopsy had come back, and that Angel had died due to a punctured lung when her assailant broke her ribs in addition to the blunt force trauma of Mr. Williams striking her in the head so hard it caused massive bleeding in her brain. They already knew that Josh had, in fact, handled the gun since he admitted to shooting Mr. Williams, so there was no need to print Josh's fingers. She said that even if they attempted to prosecute Josh for manslaughter, the best verdict they would get would be not guilty by reason of insanity OR self-defense since he was in a threatening situation. No jury in the country would find Josh guilty. Especially considering that he had never been in any trouble. The man he shot, however, had a history of being arrested many times for a variety of crimes and had just been released from prison only a few days before the incident.

Pastor Stevens found Josh in his room reading and told him he wasn't being charged with any crime and explained why. He did not tell him what his mother's official cause of death was. Josh simply shrugged and resumed reading.

CHAPTER 4

September 2, 1982

One week after the funeral, Josh was sitting silently in a lawn chair, reading, next to the Pastor's lovely home when a nice, new Cadillac pulled into the driveway. A man and woman emerged. They appeared to be a married couple in their 50s. Josh watched them as they approached the porch and rang the doorbell. They didn't seem to notice Josh as they did not acknowledge him. Pastor Stevens opened the door for them, and they walked in. A few moments later, Pastor Stevens called out to Josh and asked him to come into the house. Josh obliged and walked up the porch and into the house. When he arrived at the living room, the couple he noticed a few minutes ago were sitting on the couch. Both had smiles on their faces when they stood up to greet him.

"Joshua," the man said, "My name is Woodrow Bailey, most folks call me 'Woody' and this is my wife, Loanne. We're your aunt and uncle. Your mother was my brother, James's daughter."

Woodrow 'Woody' Bailey, 49, was a tall and gentle man. Never a harsh word. His sun-hardened face had the cracks that only hard-working outdoor men get. He had curly red hair that was almost always covered by a ball cap that had some kind of patch on it like 'CAT POWER' or 'JOHN DEERE'. He always wore jeans and boots and a button-down shirt. He was ruggedly handsome. Other than his time spent in the army, he was working on the farm. His voice was deep and husky and just loud enough for people to hear but never boisterous.

Loanne 'Lo' Bailey,49, was a striking woman. Most of the time she tied her long, black hair back. Only on select occasions, like weddings, funerals, or monthly dances with Woody, would she let her beautiful hair down. She had a sweet, calming voice and seemed to have a perpetual smile. Her beautiful brown eyes glowed.

Josh had no idea that he had relatives. His mother never spoke about her family or upbringing. When Josh would ask her about their family, she would always shrug him off and change the subject. After a while, he stopped asking.

"My mom never told me we had relatives.", Josh said.

"We thought that might be the case," Woody said, "Maybe someday we'll explain it to you. If you still want to know. We're here to take you back home with us if you want. We have a farm south of Anthony, Kansas, and we'd like you to come and live with us."

"What kind of farm?" Josh asked. "With chickens and pigs and horses?"

"It's a wheat and cattle farm," Woody said. "We raise cattle and grow wheat. We do have a few chickens we get eggs from but no pigs or horses."

Josh liked the sound of that. It felt like a good idea to leave Pleasanton and start fresh. It was scary but also exciting. He instinctively knew that staying in Pleasanton would serve as a constant reminder of his mother's absence and how she should be there with him. Plus, the razing he got at school before wouldn't compare to what they would say to him now. Besides, these people seemed nice, and they must have money since they own a Caddy.

"Okay," he said. "When do we leave?"

Loanne said, "There are some legal things we need to take care of first. Tomorrow morning we're meeting with a judge, and we've already spoken to the County Attorney and someone from child services to find out what we need to do. They're in complete agreement with us and we have proof that we're related to you so it shouldn't be a problem getting the judge to allow you to live with us."

"Everything seems to be in good order." Judge Mary Anderson declared.

Judge Anderson was seated at her desk in her chambers. A lovely woman in her 60s with graying hair and wearing a loose white blouse. She had a necklace around her neck that dropped just below her neckline. Her earrings were simple gold hoops. She exuded wisdom and understanding. She had been a judge for many years and was very good at her job. Always fair.

"Thank you, your honor," the county attorney said, "We feel that Mr. and Mrs. Bailey are more than suited to be good role models and guardians for Joshua. Plus, since we aren't pressing charges against him, we feel that this would be his best option"

Josh, Uncle Woody, and Aunt Lo (as she preferred to be called) were also seated in the judges' chambers. Sheriff Jackson was there as well as a lady who said she was with child services. The judge asked Sheriff Jackson, "What do you think, Lamar?"

Sherriff Jackson said, "It's been a rough time for him. Keeping him here in town would be, in my opinion, a bad idea. I think he should go with his relatives. Get a fresh start."

It was a cavernous room within the walls of the Linn County Courthouse. Law books surrounded the walls, and her desk was covered with papers and folders that would appear to be chaotic, but she had her system and knew exactly where everything was.

"Very well," the Judge said, "The court hereby grants custody of Joshua Bailey to Woodrow and Loanne Bailey of Anthony, Kansas in the county of Harper."

Woody and Loanne grinned widely, and a sigh of relief came from both.

The judge looked at Josh and said, "Joshua, do you understand what's happening here?"

Josh said, "I guess I'm going to live with Uncle Woody and Aunt Lo".

Lo and Woody smiled at hearing Josh refer to them that way for the first time.

"That's right", the judge replied. "But it means more than that and I want you to understand something. These two people will be your guardians until you reach the age of eighteen. They will be responsible for providing you with a home, clothing, food, and protection and making sure you become a well-adjusted and educated young man. You, Joshua, have responsibilities also. You must listen to what they tell you, abide by their rules and you must go to school. Do you understand?"

Josh responded, "Yes, ma'am"

"Good", the Judge said, "You're all free to go and the court wishes all of you the best of luck and a happy future."

Josh, Woody, and Loanne all said simultaneously, "Thank you, Judge" and they stood up to leave.

"Just one more thing, Joshua.". Judge Anderson said, "You've been given an opportunity that most boys your age and with your predicament do not get. You now have a loving home whereas you could be in a boys' home with many other orphaned boys your age or older. Do not squander this gift you have been given. You're lucky."

"I won't. I promise" Josh said.

"Terrific." The Judge said.

As the three of them left, Judge Anderson and the other remaining people in the room smiled at each other. It was nice to be doing something that didn't involve a lengthy trial with someone ending up in jail for a change. Judge Anderson said, "That right there is why I wanted to be a judge."

* * *

They hopped into the Caddy (Lo referred to it as 'hers'), Woody would drive, and Josh would sit in the back of the ultra-comfortable vehicle. It would be a four-hour drive to Anthony, but they had some stops to make first before leaving town. First, they stopped at Reverend Stevens' home to collect Josh's things. He didn't have much there. Only a few clothing items. Plus, they wanted to thank the Pastor for his kindness and to say 'good-bye' '

"Keep in touch," the Pastor said, "God bless."

As they drove away from the pastor's home, Woody asked, "Do you want to go to your house and get anything?"

Josh shook his head and said, "No. There's nothing there for me anymore."

Lo said, "We'll stop in Wichita on the way and get you some more clothes."

Josh said, "Can we stop at the cemetery before we leave town?"

Lo and Woody glanced at each other in the front seat, and Woody said, "Absolutely. I think that's a good idea."

When they arrived at the cemetery, Josh guided Woody to where his mother's gravesite was. They parked the car and got out. Josh walked slowly to his mother's grave while Lo and Woody stayed back. They knew Josh needed a moment alone. The dirt on top of the grave was still fresh and there was no grass on it yet. Josh saw the small, flat headstone that had only his mother's name on it with her birth date and date of death inscribed. He looked up and noticed most of the other headstones were upright and much larger than his mother's. He said out loud, "I'll replace your headstone someday, Mom. I promise." He took a deep breath, exhaled, and said, "I'm going away. Uncle Woody and Aunt Lo are taking me with them. I really like them. I just wish you had told me about them before." He paused then said, "I promise I'll make you proud of me, Mom. I miss you."

Woody and Lo slowly made their way over to where Josh was standing.

Lo asked, "Are you okay?'

Josh nodded 'yes' and said, "I'm ready to go."

Josh turned to make his way back to the Caddy. As he walked, he heard a bird chirping in a nearby tree. He looked up and noticed a bluejay. Then suddenly the bird flew away.

Lo and Woody took a moment to pay their respects to their long-lost niece.

Lo said, "We'll take good care of him, Angel. We promise."

* * *

They pulled out of Pleasanton and made their way south on US69 toward Ft. Scott then east on US 54 toward Wichita. Along the way, Woody and Lo tried to keep Josh's mind engaged by asking him questions about himself.

Lo asked, "What kind of food do you like?"

Josh said, "Pizza, cheeseburgers, French fries, hot dogs. I don't like vegetables except for a few of them."

"What did your mom cook for you?" Lo asked.

"She didn't really cook much. We mostly had frozen dinners and pizza. Sometimes she would make mac & cheese with little chunks of hot dogs mixed in."

Woody said, "Then you're in for a real treat. Your aunt Lo is the best cook in the entire county. You're going to have home-cooked meals every day. She makes the best-fried chicken with real mashed potatoes and gravy. We'll eat steaks and pork. We grill a lot. You're going to love her cooking. She's going to bulk you up, Buddy."

Josh asked, "What is there to do on your farm?"

"Well," Woody said, "There are tractors to drive, a combine to drive during harvest. We have two quads that we use to corral cattle. There's always something that needs to be done."

"That sounds cool." Josh said, "Can I drive all those things?"

"Of course you can." Woody said, "I'm going to teach you how to drive all of them".

"That's awesome," Josh said. "Tell me again how we're related?"

Woody looked over at Lo and said, "I'm your grandfather's brother. He was a few years older than me." He continued. "Actually, Josh, you're our grandnephew. Your mom was our niece."

Lo said, "We haven't seen your mom since her sixteenth birthday party in 1966. We lost track of her completely in 1967."

"Are my grandpa and grandma still alive?" Josh asked. "Why didn't they come for me?"

Uncle Woody said, "They were killed in a car crash in 1969. I'm sorry to have to tell you that. We are all the family you have, and you are all the family we have."

There was a moment of quiet in the Caddy then Aunt Lo asked, "What do you like to do, Josh?"

He said, "I read a lot."

Then Lo asked about sports and other things. Josh informed them that he didn't play any sports. His mom wanted him to play baseball this past summer, but he wasn't interested. Mostly, he just read books.

"What's it like on your farm?" Josh asked

Aunt Lo said, "It's a very nice house and you'll have your own bedroom and bathroom upstairs and you can decorate your bedroom any way you want."

"There are rules, though," Woody said. "The first rule is that you never lie to us about anything. We're always going to be honest with you and we fully expect you to be honest with us. Second, you are not to operate any of the equipment without my say-so. They can be very dangerous and until you know how to operate them safely, you must leave them alone. Third, you must go to school and study hard, do your homework, and get the best grades you can. We only ask that you do your very best. Fourth, listen to everything we tell you. You will have to do chores, and you will also be paid. The harder you work and the more you work, the more money you will make. Fifth, your schoolwork and chores come first. Other than your health and safety nothing is more important than your education. Lastly, we want you to have fun. This is all very new to you, and we know that, and you have much to learn. We're going to make it as fun for you as we possibly can. Do you agree to these rules?"

Josh said, "Yes, sir".

"Good. I'm hungry." Woody said. "Let's stop at the A&W in Iola and get a bacon cheeseburger and a frosty mug of root beer."

Joshua Bailey smiled for the first time in weeks.

* * *

When they arrived in Wichita, they parked the Caddy at Towne West Mall on the west side of Wichita just off Kellogg Avenue. Josh had been to a mall in Kansas City before and was excited to go to a new one. They spent a couple of hours browsing the stores and purchasing items Josh would need. New Levi's (Woody was a Wrangler's guy but Levi's were Josh's favorite). They went to Spencer's and found a bunch of t-shirts Josh liked. They had Led Zeppelin shirts AC/DC shirts and Aerosmith shirts. By the time they walked out of that store, they were carrying at least ten new T-shirts. They bought Josh a new pair of Puma's and socks. Woody gave him some cash so he could buy his own underwear. No reason for him to be embarrassed having Lo buy underwear for him.

They even went to the bookstore where Josh found some books he wanted to read. And then a stop at the music store so Josh could get some cassettes from some of his favorite bands.

Josh had never been able to go on a shopping spree before and he loved every second of it. His mom never had the money for that kind of extravagance. His mom only bought clothes for him at garage and yard sales. Never anything new. He was feeling better about life by the minute.

"Thank you for buying all this cool stuff," Josh said.

"You're welcome". Woody and Lo replied.

* * *

They departed Wichita and made their way southwest on KS highway 42, then connected with KS 2 and on into Harper where they then drove south. Josh was looking at all the fields and pastures. There were very few trees and the land was flat. He noticed several grain elevators that he could see from miles away. After they left Harper and continued south Aunt Lo said," Josh, that's Chaparral High School. That's where you'll go to school in a few years."

They continued south on highway 2 and into Anthony. Anthony, Kansas was a small town of 2,500 people. It was the county seat of Harper County, Kansas, and was connected to Oklahoma to the south. As they drove into town, Josh noticed a Pizza Hut on one side of the street. Not far from it was a small bowling alley. Across from that, there was a farm store with a big sign that read 'Fisher's Farm Store'. It was a large store and had ample parking. Some of the parking spaces were filled with pallets of bird seed, rabbit food, and a variety of other items in large bags. A couple of blocks away there was a drive-in theater. On the large marquee in front, it said, 'Now Showing: E.T. the Extra-Terrestrial'.

They arrived at the Bailey farm and Aunt Lo had promised to make her fried chicken for dinner so that made Josh even more happy. As they pulled up to the house, Josh's eyes widened with what he saw. The house that would be Josh's new home was painted a brilliant blue. It had white shutters and a large porch in front that overlooked the wheat field across the road. There were several chairs, a table set on it, and a porch swing that hung from the ceiling by two chains. Woody would tell Josh later that it had been a country schoolhouse when he and Lo bought the property. They fixed it up to make it look more like a house. Downstairs there were even remnants of the old kitchen from when it was a school. There was a huge yard, and it had two big tractors and several farm implements resting on it. There was an old barn that must have been 80 years old or more. Inside a lean-to that was attached to the shop, was a big combine that was used for wheat harvesting. They pulled the Caddy inside the building that looked more like a big shop than a garage. It was huge. When the building was a school, the large shop had been the gymnasium. It had three-grain bins inside of it that Josh would learn later stored wheat seeds that they would use to plant in the fields. There were old pickups and beat-up cars. Tools were everywhere but neatly organized. Then Josh noticed something under a tarp that he couldn't tell what it was.

He asked Woody, "What's under that tarp."

Woody said, "Go take it off and see for yourself."

Josh ran over to it and slowly removed the tarp. Underneath was an old motorcycle. It said Harley-Davidson on the gas tanks. It was black with a lot of chrome. Beautiful.

Josh said, "Is this really yours?"

Woody chuckled and said, "It sure is."

"Wow," Josh said. "It's really nice."

Woody said, "Thanks. I've had her for a long time. It's a '69 Harley-Davidson FLH"

"Can you still ride it?" Josh asked.

"Hell, yeah," Woody said. "I'm only 49 years old for Pete's sake."

Josh asked, "Will you teach me how to ride it."

Woody responded, "Sure. When you're a little bigger."

"That's so cool", Josh said.

They went inside the house from the shop, up a small flight of stairs that led into the spacious kitchen. There was a table and chairs in the kitchen. It was clean immaculate and very organized. Next to the kitchen was a dining room with a table large enough to seat six people. Next to the dining room was a spacious living room. It had a few paintings on the walls and Josh noticed several framed photographs of Woody and Lo posing together. Some were old while others looked recent. There was a large leather sofa on one wall and two recliners facing a big TV. It was a lot bigger than the TV he and his mom had back home. Along one wall he spotted an old grandfather clock.

Lo said, "Your room is upstairs. There are two of them for you to choose from. Pick whichever one you want."

Josh made his way up the stairs and found the bedroom that would be his for the foreseeable future. It had a nice bed with a comforter on it. There was a small end table with a lamp on it next to the bed and there was a closet and chest-of-drawers. The walls were blank and had been painted a sky-blue color that matched the outside of the house. He began putting away the clothes they had purchased in Wichita. Some in the drawers and some in the closet. He was meticulous about where things belonged. He hated a disorganized space. When he finished putting his new items away, he sat down on the bed and looked around his new bedroom. He sighed and said to himself, "This is awesome."

* * *

They finished dinner and Josh said, "You were right, Uncle Woody. That was the best-fried chicken and mashed potatoes I've ever had. Thank you, Aunt Lo."

Aunt Lo said, "Thank you. I'm glad you liked it." And smiled grandly.

Then she said, "On Tuesday, we need to go into town and get you enrolled for school. Labor Day is Monday, so we'll have to wait until Tuesday."

Woody and Loanne Bailey had no children of their own, so when Josh came along, they were unpracticed at the art of child-rearing. They were both happy that they could skip the diaper days and the terrible twos of raising children. They knew life ahead would be challenging, fearing their lack of experience could harm Josh, making him feel unwanted. He'd been through enough already. Loanne told Woody on their way to Pleasanton that they needed to be patient, understanding, and encouraging to Josh. She felt that she and Woody would not only be excellent guardians to him, but wonderful examples of humanity for him to observe and learn from. Woody agreed and vowed to do his very best to raise Josh to be a gentle and intelligent young man. He would teach him, lead by example, and exercise patience.

They would both succeed admirably.

CHAPTER 5

"But I don't know anyone," Josh said in a loud voice. "It's going to suck."

Woody said, "You're going to be just fine. You'll make friends quickly, you'll see."

They were all sitting at the breakfast table eating pancakes and discussing the schedule for the day. Lo said she was going to take Josh into town and get him enrolled in school.

"But what if they don't like me?", Josh asked.

Woody said, "Then that's their loss. Look, here's what you do. Wear one of your new rock and roll T-shirts. I guarantee that someone in your class will ask you about it. That solves two issues. One, it makes them break the ice and two, you'll find someone else that likes the same band you like. It's a win-win."

Josh said, "Okay".

Lo said, "Yep. And the next thing you know, you're talking

about all kinds of things. Like TV shows, movies, and girls. All kinds of stuff."

* * *

Later that morning Lo and Josh pulled up to Anthony Junior High School located not far from the main street. Made entirely out of brick, the building had been built in the 20s and it was three stories tall. The only thing that looked new was the windows. There was a flagpole out front with an American flag waving high on the pole. Green grass surrounded the building and there was no parking lot. All the cars were parked out in the street.

They entered the old building and found their way to the principal's office located at one end of the first floor. The halls were quiet since students were all in their classrooms. Painted in black on the glass of the door said, 'OFFICE', and below that read 'Regina Blackwell, principal'. They entered the office, and a pleasant-speaking lady greeted them. Lo introduced herself and Josh and stated she needed to get Josh enrolled. The lady asked what grade and Lo told her seventh. Then the nice woman told them to take a seat and Lo and Josh sat on a bench with their backs to the wall facing the rest of the office. The lady knocked on a door that also had 'Regina Blackwell' painted on it. She went inside and came out a few seconds later. She asked Lo and Josh to come on in.

They entered the office and saw a large woman sitting behind a simple wood desk. She had black hair with a silver streak and a scowl on her face. Josh smiled at himself because she reminded him of Witch Hazel from the Bugs Bunny cartoon. She said, "Come on in and have a seat".

Lo told her that Josh was her nephew who had just moved in with her and Woody and they needed to get him enrolled for classes.

It was decided after a small amount of discussion that Josh would start the next day. The semester began last week so he may have some catching up to do but it shouldn't be a problem. The principal explained some of the rules and told them that seventh-grade lockers were on the third floor, eighth-grade lockers were on the second floor and ninth-graders were on the first floor. Josh would most likely have classes on each of the floors.

She further explained to Lo how to contact the bus barn, so they knew where to pick Josh up and where to drop him off. Then she told Josh to be in her office by 8:00 tomorrow morning and she or one of the students would show him around. She would have his class schedule, books, and locker assignments when he arrived.

Lo and Josh stood thanked Ms. Blackwell and walked out.

On the way home, Lo asked, "What did you think of the principal?"

Josh said, "Did you ever see the Bugs Bunny cartoon that had Witch Hazel in it?"

Lo chuckled, "Yeah".

"She looks just like her".

* * *

Later that evening, Woody, Lo, and Josh were at the kitchen table and had just finished eating dinner.

There was a moment of silence. Then Woody looked at Josh and said, "There will be kids at your school that are going to ask where you're from and a bunch of other personal questions. You can tell them whatever you want but I would suggest not telling them about what happened in Pleasanton. It's none of their damn business. Just tell them your mom passed away and that you live with us now. They don't need to know any more than that. If they ask how your mom died just ignore it and change the subject. We know a lot of the parents of the kids you'll be going to school with and when they hear about you, they'll be asking us questions too. We're only going to tell them what I told you to say."

Josh nodded and said, "Okay".

* * *

September 7th, 1982

The yellow and black school bus arrived at the Bailey farm promptly at 7:00 a.m. the next morning. The driver opened the door and Josh looked back at the house. He could see Aunt Lo watching from the kitchen window. He sighed heavily and made his way up the steps to where the driver was sitting. The driver was a rotund man in his 60s. He wore overalls and had on a WSU baseball cap.

He said, "Are you Josh?"

Josh nodded and the driver said, "I'm Gus. Good to meet

you. Find a seat somewhere. We'll stop at the grade school first and then the Junior High."

The bus was only about half full and Josh made his way nervously down the aisle. The other kids were silent and looking him over. He had on his new Puma sneakers, and denim shorts and he was wearing his new Led Zeppelin T-shirt that proudly said 'LED ZEPPELIN' and below that had what looked like drawings of the faces of the band. Jimmy, Robert, John Paul and of course 'Bonzo' Bonham. Carrying a nearly empty backpack and a small bag that held his lunch, he found an empty seat near the back of the bus placed his backpack on the seat, and sat down.

Gus placed the bus in gear, and they drove away. By the time they got into town, the bus had become livelier. The other kids began talking to each other and the farther the bus traveled the noisier it got with chatter.

Josh remained silent all the way to the school.

Josh was in the school office before 8:00 sitting on the same bench that he and Aunt Lo had sat on the previous day. The nice lady behind the counter told Josh to come and get his books, class schedule, and another piece of paper that had his locker number on it and the combination for the lock. He placed the books in his backpack and sat back down. Suddenly, Ms. Blackwell emerged from her office. She said, "Good morning. Give me just a second and I'll find someone to show you around and help you to your first class."

She opened the office door and peered out into the hall

which was nearly empty with students going to their classrooms. Then she noticed a student who was scrambling to get to her classroom on time.

Witch Hazel (as Josh would refer to her) yelled out. "Lisa! Lisa Fisher come in here, please".

Josh turned to see the cutest girl he had ever seen. Her blond hair was tied in two braided pig tails, and she was wearing shorts and sneakers. Her blue eyes sparkled. She had on a nice blouse and was carrying her backpack.

Witch Hazel introduced them and asked Lisa to show Josh where his first class was and where his locker was.

Lisa said, "Okay. Let's go"

The two of them made their way to the stairs and started their long climb to the third floor. She asked Josh where he was from, and he told her he was from a small town near Kansas City that his mother died recently, and he was living with his Uncle Woody and Aunt Lo.

Lisa said," Woody and Loanne Bailey?"

Josh nodded and she said, "I know them. They're good friends of my mom and dad."

Lisa went on to explain how the school was laid out and which grades were on which floor.

Josh stopped her and said, "Yeah, Hazel explained it to me yesterday."

Lisa looked at him quizzically and said, "Hazel?".

Josh said, "Yeah. Ms. Blackwell. I call her Hazel because she looks like Witch Hazel from the Bugs Bunny cartoon"

Lisa laughed, "She does, doesn't she? That's hilarious."

She showed him to his locker and following the

instructions he was given, was able to open it with no problem. Then she checked his class schedule showed him where his first class was and explained the classroom numbers. The first number of the classroom indicated which floor the classroom was on. Josh had already figured that out, but he didn't want to interrupt her tour, and he liked the sound of her voice.

They finally reached Josh's first class, and he thanked her for her help. She told him he was welcome, and she'd see him around.

Josh said softly to himself, "I hope so."

Every classroom he went to was the same. Plain, dull walls. The windows were open in all of them because the old building had no air conditioning, and each room had a box fan circulating hot air. Plus, every teacher in every class felt it necessary to introduce Josh as a new student and everyone should welcome him, blah, blah, blah.

When lunch time arrived, Josh found his way to the lunchroom. The long tables with attached seats could be folded up and moved easily on wheels. It wasn't any different than his old school in Pleasanton.

Josh found a spot separate from the other students and began eating the chicken sandwich that Aunt Lo had made up for him. Most of the other students had trays of food they got from the kitchen and were talking and eating. The walls echoed the voices of the noisy Jr. High kids.

Then out of nowhere, a guy with long straight hair came

up to Josh. He was wearing a Van Halen T-shirt and shorts. The guy said to Josh, "Zepplin fan, huh?"

Josh looked down at his T-shirt and said, "What gave it away?"

The kid laughed and said, "I know. Stupid question. Your name's Josh, right?"

Josh nodded and the guy said, "I'm Lance. I saw you this morning. We're in the same homeroom. Where are you from?"

Josh said, "Everyone keeps asking me that."

He explained to Lance the same thing he did with Lisa earlier in the day.

"Do you like it here?", Lance asked.

"It's too soon to say yet. So far everyone's been nice except for the principal, I don't like her. She gives me a bad feeling."

Lance said, "Yeah, she's scary. We joke about her all the time."

Josh said, "I'm already calling her Hazel like Witch Hazel."

Lance laughed and said, "Like in the cartoon, right?"

"Exactly".

Lance said, "Did you ever notice that when Witch Hazel runs, her hair pins are flying out of her hair and they just hang there?"

They both laughed and Josh said, "Yeah, that's funny."

Lance said, "When you get done eating, you want to go play dodgeball?"

Josh said, "Sure. Where?"

Lance told him where the school gym was and when they finished eating, they made their way to the gym.

They walked into the gym and sat on the bleachers. Josh

had never been asked to play games or join a team before. He was very nervous. Lance asked if he knew how to play dodgeball, and Josh told him he did. He knew the rules.

A few minutes later a guy who Josh figured was a freshman announced that it was the seventh graders' turn to play. At junior high, the classes were split into two groups, Seventh A and seventh B. The same for eighth grade and the freshmen. Josh and Lance were in seventh A, and they would be playing against seventh B. They made their way onto the court.

The balls were lined up in a row in the center of the court. Both teams were at either end of the gym and the referee (the same freshman who made the announcement) blew his whistle and both teams ran to grab the balls. There were seven balls altogether, four of them Josh's team snagged and the other three were picked up by the opposing team. Balls were flying back and forth across the gym. Some were caught which meant the person who threw it was out and some connected and bounced off the opponent causing that player to be out. Josh managed to catch one and threw it back to the other side and nailed a kid who was looking the wrong way and didn't see it coming. Two outs. Josh glanced over just in time to see Lance get hit. It went back and forth for several minutes until it came down to just Josh and another kid on the other side. That kid was big for a seventh-grader. Red hair and freckles. Very tough looking. Josh picked up a loose ball and held it tight watching his opponent closely. There were two balls on Josh's side including the one he was holding, the other kid had five to choose from. Josh was outnumbered and much smaller than the red-headed kid. Josh threw his ball and missed and not taking his eyes off his opponent ran to get the other remaining ball. The big kid threw hard at Josh, but Josh was able to step out of the way. He picked up a ball and held onto it. Josh stood waiting for the guy to throw, ball in hand. When the guy threw his ball, Josh quickly dropped the ball he had and caught the ball that was thrown at him. Out!

The students sitting in the bleachers were shocked. No one had ever beaten this guy before. The guys from Josh's team all cheered and ran to him. Patting him on the back and congratulating him.

All the students walked out of the gym on their way to their next class except for one person. Lisa Fisher stood silently and unnoticed and watched Josh as he walked out of the gym with his new friend, Lance.

* * *

The bus pulled up in front of the house and Josh stood up and strolled to the front. Gus said, "See you tomorrow,"

Josh said, "Not if I see you first." And quickly walked down the bus's steps and started toward the house. He looked over at the yard and noticed that one of the tractors was gone. He walked in the front door and was greeted warmly by Aunt Lo.

She said, "How was your first day?"

Josh smiled and said, "I made a friend.'

"You did? Already?"

"And I met a girl. She said that she knows you and Uncle Woody."

Lo asked her name and Josh responded, "Lisa Fisher."

Lo smiled and said, "We know her and her family. We've

been friends with them for a long time." She said, then she turned away and still smiling asked, "What did you think of her?"

Josh said, "She's a cutie."

Josh related to her about Lance and what happened during the dodgeball game. Then he asked, "Where's the other tractor at?"

Lo explained that Woody was working the field across the road.

She asked, "Do you have any homework?"

Josh shook his head 'no' and Lo walked to the two-way radio they had set up in the kitchen. She keyed the mic and asked for Woody. Woody responded and Lo told him that Josh was home. Woody said, "Okay. I'll be there in a couple of minutes."

She turned to Josh and said, "Woody will be coming up soon. Why don't you go across the road and meet him in the field?"

Josh said, "Okay" and made his way out the door and across the road.

The field was surrounded by barbed wire but there was an open gate about 50 feet away. Josh wandered over to the gate and a few moments later he could see the big tractor working its way around the field. The tractor was green with yellow stripes. It had eight huge tires, and light smoke was billowing out of its exhaust stack. Woody pulled up to where Josh was and lowered the engine and opened the door to the massive machine. Woody called down to him and said, "climb on up here." Josh grabbed the handles and stepped up the six or so steps to the cab of the tractor. There was just enough room for him to sit to the side of Woody. Woody placed the tractor in gear, revved the engine back up, and continued with his work.

"How was school?" Woody asked.

Josh told him about Lance and what happened at the dodgeball game. Woody smiled and nodded his head.

"Sounds like you had an interesting first day," he said.

"You could say that".

Josh asked what Woody was doing with the tractor. Woody explained that they were getting the fields ready to plant wheat and that he was pulling what he called a spring tooth. Josh watched fascinated as the implement stirred the ground, and he watched how Uncle Woody operated the tractor and the controls. They did a full round of the field and Woody stopped the tractor and said, "You ready to give it a go?"

Josh said, "Me? You want me to drive this thing?"

Woody said, "Yep. You're going to learn sometime. Might as well be now".

Woody got out of the seat so Josh could sit in it. He explained all the controls and what they did. He showed him how to put it in the correct gear and how to keep it straight while keeping an eye on the spring tooth. Soon they were moving, and Josh was nervous. He didn't want to make any mistakes. They did a couple of rounds of the field and Josh was becoming more comfortable.

Woody said, "Stop here and let me out". Josh stopped the tractor, and Woody told him he was on his own. "I want you to do three rounds by yourself then stop. If you have any questions or problems, just get on the radio and holler for me. I'll be in the pickup watching. It has a radio in it too."

Woody climbed out of the monster machine and watched as Josh revved the engine back up and drove off. He could see the excitement on Josh's face as he drove away.

Josh was focused on what he was doing. Paying attention to everything the implement was doing and where the tractor was going.

He said out loud, "This is the coolest thing ever."

It had been an amazing day for young Josh Bailey.

* * *

October 1st, 1982

"Did you see the new J. Geils video, Centerfold?" Lance asked Josh.

He and Josh were in between classes talking and watching the girls. Josh said, "I like it when the drummer hits the snare drum at the end and all this milk comes flying out of it."

Lance said, "That's pretty cool."

"Did you see that?", Josh asked Lance. "That dude just shoved Stevie away from the water fountain while he was drinking."

"Yeah, that's Sam Blackwell, Witch Hazel's kid," Lance replied.

Sam Blackwell was a menacing eighth grader. He had gotten away with many bullying incidents since his mother was the principal at Anthony Jr. High. Bigger than most of the kids at the school, completely spoiled and narcissistic. The very kind of person Josh hated. As Sam bent down to get a sip from the fountain, Josh came running over to him and shoved him away just like Sam had done to Stevie a second before. The push was just enough to give Josh room between Sam and the fountain.

"You little punk,", Sam yelled. "I'm going to beat your ass."

Josh stood defiantly facing Sam. "No, you won't." Without taking his eyes off Sam, Josh said to Stevie who was behind Josh, "Go ahead and get your drink of water, Stevie. I'll watch this jerk."

Sam clinched his fist and took a swing at Josh; Josh dodged the wild swing and instantly punched Sam in the gut. Sam bent over; his breath was knocked out of him. Just then, Josh felt two large hands grab him by the shoulders and fling him to the floor of the mostly empty hallway. He looked up to see Witch Hazel standing over him.

"My office, Mr. Bailey, right now," she said. "The rest of you get to class."

"What about Sam?" Josh asked.

"You let me worry about him, you just go to my office."

The phone rang at the Bailey farm and Lo answered. She listened for a moment and said, "Are you sure you want to do that?" A few more seconds went by, and Lo said, "We'll be right there." She turned to Woody who was sitting at the kitchen table eating lunch and said, "That was Regina Blackwell, she said Josh was fighting and that she's suspending him from school.

Woody said, "Let's go."

* * *

Uncle Woody and Aunt Lo walked into the office to see Josh sitting on the bench near the office counter. Lo asked Josh, "Are you alright?"

Josh nodded and Woody asked him, "What happened?"

Just as Josh was about to speak, Regina Blackwell stepped out of her office and told them, "Come into my office."

Woody said, "In a second."

Regina responded, "No, right now,"

Woody glared at her and said, "Don't you dare talk to me like I'm one of your students. Who the hell do you think you are? We want to talk to Josh first. You can wait."

Woody asked Josh again what had happened, and Josh told him the whole story. Seeing Sam shove Stevie, him shoving Sam and Sam trying to hit him and him punching Sam in the gut, and then "she grabbed me from behind and threw me to the floor".

"Did anyone else see it happen?" Woody asked.

"Yeah, Lance was there. He saw the whole thing."

Woody turned to look at Regina and said, "We're ready to talk now."

They all entered Regina's office and took seats. Regina at her cheap wooden desk and Lo, Woody, and Josh in chairs across from her.

Regina said, "Josh, you wait outside."

Woody said, "Stay where you are, Josh." Then to Regina,

"Where do you get off grabbing our nephew and tossing him onto the floor?"

She said, "He was out of control. I did what I had to do."

Lo said, "I highly doubt he was out of control. All you had to do was step between them and send them both to your office. Where's the other one? The one who started the whole thing?"

"Not that it's any of your business but I sent him to his class," Regina responded.

"Why isn't he in here with us?" Woody asked.

Josh said, "He's her son, Uncle Woody. I bet you can guess why."

Woody and Lo were fuming. Woody said to Regina, "Here's what you're going to do. You're going to apologize to our nephew. Then you're going to rescind his suspension and expel that boy of yours."

"I won't do any such thing," Regina said, "I'm the principal here and I can dole out punishment as I see fit. Your nephew was fighting and that's grounds for suspension for five days."

Woody said, "So we'll take that as a 'no'?"

"That's right", Regina said.

Woody stood up, "You may want to start packing up your office. You're not going to need it much longer."

Lo pointed a finger at Regina and said, "You think I don't remember you from when you used to pick on me? I remember it all. I know who you are, and I know what you're all about and if you ever lay a hand on my nephew again, I'll knock your damn teeth out, Bitch."

As they were leaving, the bell rang for the kids to switch classes. The hallway filled with students and Lance saw the three of them walking toward the front door of the school. He ran up to them and asked Josh, "What happened?"

Josh said, "Five days suspension."

Woody asked Lance, "Josh said you saw the whole thing, did you?"

Lance said, "Yes, sir"

Woody said, "We may need you to verify what you saw later."

"No problem" Lance replied.

* * *

"I'm sorry you had to come to the school.", Josh said. He was sitting in the back of the Caddy staring out the window and watching the wheat fields and pastures go by.

Woody glanced up at the rear-view mirror and said, "You have nothing to be sorry about. You did the right thing."

Josh said, "I couldn't just let that punk get away with what he did. Stevie's a good guy and it pissed me off. He's in special ed and I felt bad for him."

Lo said, "We're not upset with you. We're angry with Witch Hazel."

Woody looked at her questionably and said, "Witch Hazel?"

"That's what Josh calls Regina," Lo said,

Woody laughed and said, "Here's what we're going to do…"

"This is what needs to happen," Woody told the board of education the following Monday. "Our witnesses and I have explained the situation and what occurred. As we see it, these are your options. One, you rescind our nephew, Josh's suspension and remove it from his record. Two, you expel Sam Blackwell for the remainder of the year and three, you terminate Regina Blackwell as principal effective immediately. If you refuse to do any of those things, we will be forced to react in a way that will not look good for this entire district. That will include having Regina Blackwell arrested for child abuse and calling every news outlet in Wichita to report that the board of education in Anthony chose to protect an abusive principal over protecting your students. You need to make that decision right here, right now. No tabling it. No closed-door sessions. My wife and I are confident that you'll do the right thing, but we are fully prepared to take this further if need be."

The four men and three women of the school board looked down at Woody from their raised platform. Each had a name plate in front of them. The well-lit room was silent with only a few people in attendance. Some appeared shocked at what they had just heard. Others were smiling. Lance, Stevie, and both their sets of parents were there. Lance and Stevie had told the board what they saw and what happened at the water fountain earlier during the meeting. Josh and Lo were sitting quietly.

Suddenly a lady at the far end of the platform spoke to the other board members, she said, "I've known Woody and Loanne Bailey for a long time. They're both wonderful people and they have an outstanding reputation among all of us here in town. It is not likely that they would make any of this up. They are well-liked and contribute much. I, for one, am in complete agreement with Mr. Bailey. Therefore, I move that we abide by and agree with their requests that Joshua Bailey's suspension be removed and that his record show the same. Also, that Sam Blackwell be expelled from school for the remainder of the year and lastly, Regina Blackwell be terminated effective immediately"

Simultaneously, four of the board members stated, "I second the motion."

The Superintendent said, "All those in favor say 'Aye'.

"Aye," they all responded.

Woody looked around at all of them and said, "Thank you. You did the right thing."

As they left the building and walked toward the Caddy, Josh asked, "Who was that lady that spoke up and said she knew you guys?"

Lo and Woody smiled and looked at each other, Lo said. "That was Nancy Fisher. Lisa Fisher's mom."

* * *

The following day, students were elated when they heard what happened the night before at the board meeting. Word traveled fast in Anthony and all the kids were thanking Josh for standing up against Ms. Blackwell.

"I don't like this attention." He told Lance at lunch. "I wish everyone would just forget about it. I really didn't do anything."

Lance said, "Come on. You're a hero to everyone here. You

made Witch Hazel go away and you stood up to Sam. Noone has ever done that before."

"I was only trying to protect a weaker kid from an asshat. That's all. She brought that all on herself. If it wasn't me, someone else would've done it sooner or later."

Just then, Lisa Fisher, along with her best friend Becky, approached the two comrades. Lisa looked better than ever. Her friend, Becky was a petite girl with brown hair that she had placed in pigtails like her friend. Lisa said, "Hey, Josh. My mom told me what your uncle did last night. I wish I'd seen it. It must have been awesome".

Josh said, "Uncle Woody's the best. Your mom did a lot of it. I didn't know she was your mom until Uncle Woody and Aunt Lo told me after it was all over."

"Yep," she said, "That's my mom. I'll see you guys later."

Josh watched her and Becky walk away and Lance started to laugh.

"What?" Josh said.

"Dude, you are so in love with her," Lance said laughing.

"No more than you are with Becky," Josh said. "I saw the way you were looking at her. At least I admit my crush."

CHAPTER 6

April 2nd, 1984

"Happy birthday, Josh," Aunt Lo and Uncle Woody said as Josh approached the breakfast table.

Aunt Loanne had prepared Josh's favorite breakfast of scrambled eggs, bacon, and hash browns.

"I can't believe it's been almost two years since we brought you home with us." Uncle Woody said.

Aunt Lo asked, "Are you still happy here?'

Josh said, "I love it here. I have friends here; I get to drive the tractors and ride the quads. You guys have been so good to me. I really appreciate it."

Woody said, "We're glad you're happy. You're doing very well in school; you work hard, and I don't think I've ever heard you complain about anything. When you get home from school today, I've got something I want to show you."

* * *

It had been a terrific year and a half since Josh arrived at the farm. He and Lance spent many hours riding the quads in the nearby pasture on Saturdays. Sometimes, Josh would stay at Lance's house and listen to him play his guitar. Lance was getting better and better at his playing. He would dream of being in a rock band someday.

Josh's life had changed so much since his time in Pleasanton. He was no longer bullied. He had good friends including Lance. He had grown a good eight inches, and he was bigger and stronger thanks to Aunt Lo's fantastic cooking. Plus, he got to see and talk to Lisa at school every day. She was very friendly to him.

* * *

When he arrived home from school that day, he found Uncle Woody in the shop. Josh said, "What did you want to show me, Uncle Woody?"

Woody said, "Get in the truck, Josh."

Josh did as he was told, and he saw Uncle Woody coming toward the truck with a gun case. Woody placed the case in the toolbox that sat on the truck bed, climbed into the driver's seat, and drove down the road to the pasture a quarter mile away. They had sold the steers and heifers last month, so the pasture was empty. The ground was rough and not suitable for planting wheat. It had a small creek bed going through it and a couple of lonely trees on it.

While they drove, Woody said, "Did I ever tell you about my time in the Army?"

"Not much," Josh said. "You only said you were a soldier when you were younger."

Woody said, "I was drafted when I turned eighteen in 1951. I did very well at boot camp, and they decided to train me as a sniper. I was a good shot. Then they sent me to Korea. My job was to take out as many enemy soldiers as possible to help keep my fellow soldiers safe before they took a hill or village. I was good at it...very good. I killed at least ten North Korean or Chinese soldiers that I know of. We would often have to lie in the mud and tall grass. The idea was to shoot and move undetected. One shot, then move. I also learned hand-to-hand combat. Where to strike a person that would do the most damage and how to protect ourselves from our combatant."

"Wow," Josh said. "That sounds exciting."

"It was", Woody said, "But it was also very hard. I hated seeing my friends die and being away from your Aunt Lo was no fun either. I missed her badly while I was gone. All I wanted to do was survive and get back home so I could marry her."

When they arrived at the spot Woody had chosen, they got out of the pickup and Woody grabbed the gun case. He opened it and withdrew a rifle. "This is a Springfield M1903 rifle." He said. "This type of rifle was used in WWII by a lot of snipers and in Korea too. It's a bolt-action rifle and is very accurate in the hands of a skilled sniper. It fires a .30-06 round and is accurate up to 400 yards with the scope I have attached to it. It holds 5 rounds." Woody demonstrated how to load the weapon and work the bolt. Then he stood still and brought the rifle up to his shoulder. "See that tree there 300 yards on the left?"

Josh said he did, and Woody aimed the rifle, peered through the scope, and fired the shot. The bullet hit the tree trunk dead center. Woody said, "Give it a try." He handed the rifle to Josh and explained how to chamber the next round with the bolt. He said, "One of the best things about a bolt action rifle is that, unlike an automatic weapon, the spent casing doesn't come out until you chamber the next round. Automatic or semi-automatics discharge the spent shell immediately after the previous round is fired."

Josh raised the rifle to his shoulder and looked through the scope at the same tree Woody had shot at. He took a breath and exhaled, squeezing the trigger as he was instructed. The round hit the tree perfectly.

Woody said, "You're a natural. Good shot. Now there's something I need to tell you, Josh. Look at me because this is important. You only get one shot at life and takes only one shot to end a life. You need to remember that. Make the most of the one shot you have in life and if you absolutely must, use only one shot to defend yourself or to protect those who cannot defend themselves. Understand?"

Josh nodded and said, "I'll remember."

* * *

Over the next several months, Woody would also teach Josh about self-defense and fighting. He showed him the various places on the human body that were susceptible to causing the most injury and subduing his attacker. Woody said, "Nose, throat, crotch, and legs. A good punch to a person's nose will blind them temporarily, a jab to the throat will mess up their ability to breathe, a kick to the groin will cause immediate pain, and taking out a leg will put them on the ground. If you've ever seen a street fight, most people swing their fists and connect with their opponent's jaw. It's effective but not as much as the other points. Also, most people are right-handed, so be aware that they'll try to use their right hand first. Always look them in the eye. Most of the time their eyes will give away what their next move will be. Never take your eyes off them."

They would spend many hours sparring during that time. Josh enjoyed learning these new skills and became very fast with his fists. Between shooting and sparring, Josh would get better and better at these newfound abilities. More importantly, his confidence in himself was increasing.

Woody would tell Josh more than once, "You don't need to go looking for trouble, it'll find you soon enough. Defend yourself and those you care about but do not go on the offensive and start shit. Only use what you're learning for defense."

CHAPTER 7

April 2nd, 1986

"Good morning, birthday boy", Aunt Lo said as Josh took his seat at the breakfast table.

"Thanks," Josh replied.

"How does it feel to be 16?" Woody asked.

"Okay, I guess", Josh said.

Aunt Lo placed a wrapped box in front of Josh. She said, "Open it."

Josh quickly tore the paper off the box, opened the box, and inside was a black ballcap with Harley-Davidson imprinted on the front. Josh smiled and said, "Thanks Uncle Woody, Aunt Lo. I love it."

Woody said, "Would you do me a favor and go out into the shop and bring me a Philips head screwdriver?"

"Sure", Josh replied. He plopped his new hat on his head, got up from the table, and walked toward the steps that led down to the shop. Lo and Woody quickly stood up and walked fast to follow Josh. Lo was carrying her camera out of Josh's view. When they got to the shop, they saw Josh looking for the screwdriver. He hadn't noticed the new tarp at the other end of the shop.

Woody said, "Hey, what's that over there?"

"Where?" Josh said.

"Under that tarp," Woody said pointing at the tarp.

Josh turned and looked. "I don't know. What is it?"

Lo said, "Why don't you go find out?"

Josh raced over to the tarp and quickly removed it from whatever it was covering. Immediately his eyes widened at what he saw. "Is this mine?" he asked.

Woody said, "Yep. She's a 1984 Harley Davidson Softail and she's all yours. Happy birthday, Buddy"

The bike was black with a lot of chrome. "I can't believe it. Thank you, thank you, thank you."

"You're welcome." Aunt Lo said as she took a photo of Josh grinning from ear to ear and admiring his new bike.

Woody said, "We decided that since you've worked so hard the past four years, kept up with your schoolwork, and stayed out of trouble, you earned it. We believe in rewarding hard work."

"This is the best birthday gift ever." Josh said, "I can't wait to ride it."

"What's stopping you?", Woody said. "It's your bike to ride. You've spent enough time on mine riding around. But like always you must wear your helmet, and you need to get your motorcycle permit and your endorsement on your current license."

"I will. Right away." Josh said.

"Four years. Where does the time go?", Aunt Lo said. "You've grown up so much. I bet you're a foot taller than you were when you came here. Plus, all that food you put away has made you bigger too."

Josh had experienced a major growth spurt, and his voice had changed too. He was no longer that skinny kid he was four years ago. Now he was 5'5" tall. Lean and muscular. Woody had taught him how to drive, ride the motorcycle, and work the fields like an old pro. He worked hard and continued to read a lot of books. His book choices had changed also. Now he was reading crime novels and thrillers and the occasional courtroom dramas. When asked why he read so much, he always replied, "I like learning new things and about other places and people."

Chaparral High School sat between the towns of Anthony and Harper surrounded by wheat fields. It had been built in the 60s, had its own water tower, and was accessible by students from all over Harper County. Josh was now in the second semester of his sophomore year. He could still be seen hanging out with Lance and a few other people with similar interests. But Lance was his best friend. They made each other laugh. They would often argue over which band was the best or which guitar player was best or drummer. They would attend football games on Friday nights in the fall and basketball games during winter. He wouldn't admit to anyone that he was mostly interested in watching Lisa cheerlead. He had trouble keeping his eyes off her and her gorgeous blonde, wavy hair and those legs...wow, those legs. After the games, they would sometimes go to the lake and socialize with their classmates. Josh didn't always go with them but occasionally Lance would convince him to go. He didn't like seeing Lisa with other guys and was too shy to ask her out himself. They were friendly. Always said "hello" in the hallways at school and she would ask him how things were going. She was friendly to him but then she was friendly to everyone. Other than spending time with Lance, Josh would mostly keep to himself reading or doing homework. He was mostly invisible to the other students. So, when he rode up to the school on his Harley for the first time, he turned some heads. Including Lisa's.

Lance saw him first and said to everyone around him standing in front of the building. "Holy shit. Look at this."

Everyone turned and in rode Josh with his Harley, pipes rumbling. He parked the bike and dismounted. Lance ran up to him. He said, "Dude, where'd you get this?"

"Uncle Woody and Aunt Lo gave it to me for my birthday. Pretty badass, huh?"

Lance said, "I don't think there's ever been a student at Chaparral with a Harley before."

"Well, there is now," Josh said.

Lisa and Becky walked up, and Lisa said, "Hey, Josh. Nice bike."

He responded, "Thanks".

She said. "I knew you were getting it. Woody kept it hidden at our store since last week."

"Nice of you to keep it a secret from me." He quipped.

"I didn't want to spoil the surprise. When do I get a ride?", Lisa asked.

Josh said, "The minute you break up with Cole".

Lisa smiled, "Well, maybe someday. See you guys later." And walked away.

Lance said, "It may be a while but eventually she'll come around."

"I can't wait to get her on this bike," Josh said. "Her arms wrapped around me while I was rubbing her leg. That's the dream, buddy."

* * *

At most high schools, the male students were divided into several groups or cliques. At Chaparral, there were the 'Nerds', the 'Jocks', the 'gearheads', the 'rednecks', and the 'freaks' or 'dopers'. Some of those groups would be multi-layered. Some of the rednecks were jocks and some of the nerds were freaks and so on. Each group had their own shared interests. It was well known by most that the 'jocks' were the most popular. They were the football players, basketball players, wrestlers, etc. The girls really didn't have classifications like the guys did. Certainly not as many of them and it was difficult to distinguish them separately or place them in a specific group. As far as Lance and Josh could tell, they were all pretty much the same. All the girls, it seemed to Josh, were very pleasant and for the most part, attractive.

"What's with these new hairstyles?" Lance asked Josh.

"I think they call it "big hair," Josh said.

Lance said, "They all look like they placed an M-80 on top of their heads and lit it."

"They sure do go through a lot of cans of hairspray. That's for sure." Josh retorted.

They were standing in the hallway watching the girls walk by between classes like they did every day. Then they heard a voice behind them say, "Bailey."

Josh turned and saw standing 10 feet away, Cole Jensen, Lisa's star quarterback boyfriend. He was a Junior, a year older than Josh and Lance but already he had been the starting quarterback for the Roadrunner's football team. He was the same size as Josh. Not big but not short either. He had neatly trimmed brown hair and was always dressed as if he were the king of the world, and he thought he was also. He stood with three of his fellow jocks and said to Josh, "Come over here, I want to talk to you."

Josh looked around, pointed at himself, and said, "Me?"

"Yeah, you. Come over here." Cole said.

"I'm sorry," Josh said. "I misunderstood you. I thought you must be talking to someone who takes orders from you. I'm not that guy. If you want me, you come to me."

Cole and his three goons walked to where Josh and Lance were standing, Cole didn't stop until he was face-to-face inches away.

"Listen you little fuck", Cole said steaming. "You need to leave Lisa alone. You're not allowed to talk to her"

"Excuse me?", Josh said. "Are you seriously giving me another order?"

"Yes, I am". Cole said. "You think since you have that Harley that you're some kind of badass."

"Apparently you didn't hear me the first time", Josh said, "I don't take orders from you or anyone else. Now, if Lisa wants me to stop talking to her, she can tell me herself which I know she won't do."

A small crowd began to circle what was clearly becoming a confrontation.

"You need to watch your ass, Bailey," Cole said.

Josh said, "Why? Is there something wrong with it?"

"You know what I mean", Cole said.

Josh said, "I'll tell you what. If Lisa decides to stop talking to me, then and only then will I abide by her wishes. Not yours." Josh continued, "Don't make the mistake of thinking you scare me. I assure you, you don't. However, I am a little afraid of your breath. You need a tic tac, Man."

Some members of the group circling the action laughed at Josh's remark. Especially Lance.

"Let me ask you something. Do you sign Lisa's paycheck?" Josh asked. "Because the last I knew, she worked for her dad at their store. I didn't know you were her boss. You're not my boss or anyone else's for all I know. You may want to reevaluate your position here."

"Listen, you fucking Nerd," Cole said. "I will mess you up."

Josh laughed and said, "Did you just call me a nerd? If that was supposed to be an insult, you failed. I'd rather be known as a nerd than a jock any day. Now that I think about it, I'm a combination of three cliques. Sometimes I'm a redneck because I live and work on a farm. Other times I think I'm a freak because those guys are laid back and mellow and other times I feel like a nerd because I read a lot. I'm a Redfreaknerd." He continued, "You think you can "mess me up" as you say, but you can't, and you won't. You won't try it here in school anyway. You're stupid but not stupid enough to risk getting kicked out of school for fighting. You'd have to throw the first punch, which you'll miss, and then be embarrassed by having a "nerd", as you called me, break your damn nose."

Just then Mr. Winkler stepped out of his nearby classroom and noticed the crowd. He walked between a couple of the onlookers and said, "What's the problem, Mr. Jensen? Mr. Bailey?"

Cole took a step back and said, "No problem. Just having a friendly conversation with Bailey here."

"Honestly, Mr. Winkler". Josh said, "It wasn't much of a conversation at all. Cole here doesn't have the mental capacity to carry on a conversation. So, there's no problem here, sir."

Cole turned and walked away with his posse and the crowd scattered and went about going to their next class.

Lance said, "Dude, that was hilarious."

"He's an egotistical ass and thinks he runs this school because he's the big, bad quarterback. Well, he doesn't run me, and he doesn't scare me either. I'll tell you something else, if that asshole ever hurts Lisa, he's going to feel a lot of pain. I promise you that."

After classes ended for the day, Lisa caught up with Josh getting on his bike. She said, "I heard about you and Cole. I'm sorry."

"You don't have anything to be sorry about. He's

responsible for his own actions. I've been instructed by him not to talk to you. What are your thoughts on that?" Josh asked.

"My thoughts are that I'll talk to whoever I want," Lisa said defiantly. "I told him that if he wants to keep dating me, he needs to leave you alone and I'll talk to anyone I want including you."

"That's good to hear," Josh said. "I don't think I'd enjoy not talking to you or seeing you."

"I wouldn't like that either," Lisa said.

Josh said, "He's trouble, Lisa. I'm not going to tell you who you can and can't date. That's not my place, but I will say that I feel a bad vibe coming from him. Just be careful. He's dangerous and unpredictable. Trust me when I tell you I've seen his type before when I was a kid."

"I'll take that under advisement. Thanks" Lisa said.

"One more thing, just so you know," Josh said. "If he ever hurts you, he'll be feeling a lot of pain brought on by me. He's underestimated what I'm capable of and I can read him like a book. A children's book at that."

Late May 1987.

One year and two months later was the last day of now seventeen-year-old Josh's junior year. Only one more year to go and he would graduate. During the past year, Cole would not follow through on his threats and Josh would continue to talk to Lisa and she would talk to him. Cole had graduated and from what Josh was told, had received a scholarship to play football at some community college somewhere in Kansas. Josh didn't care where; he was happy enough knowing Cole would be leaving.

On this night, the last day of school, several of the juniors and seniors had all gathered at the lake. On the backside of the lake, there was a small, wooded area that had enough room for several cars to park. There were keg parties there often during the spring and summer. Josh didn't like being around the drunk teenagers but since this was his last day as a junior and Lance convinced him to go, he went. He spent the evening sitting on the tailgate of Woody's pickup drinking his bottle of Coke and watching the shenanigans. Occasionally a classmate would stop and talk to him and then stagger away. Most of the participants were carrying red cups full of beer. He saw a few people smoking joints and laughing. Some of the girls were dancing with each other and falling down a lot, laughing the entire time. Loud music was blaring from someone's car stereo. Then something caught his eye. Coming up on his right was Lance and he was hand in hand with Becky Simons. Becky was still a petite girl with a button nose. She had medium-length, brown hair. Her small stature was no match for her boisterous voice. She reveled in sarcasm and was a lot of fun to hang out with. Josh always admired her ability to 'not give a fuck' about what folks thought of her. She and Lisa had grown up together and were very close. As they approached, Josh couldn't conceal his smile at seeing them together. They each had a red cup in their free hands.

"Well look at you two," Josh exclaimed. "This is new. How ya doing, Becky?"

Becky replied excitedly, "I'm wonderful. How are you?"

Josh still smiling said, "I can't complain." Josh wagged his finger between the pair and said, "I like this. The two of you all cozied up together. It's a good thing to see."

Lance took a sip of his beer and said, "I've been waiting for this since the sixth grade."

Becky back-handed Lance in the chest and quipped, "What? Why did you take so long?"

"I honestly don't know, Beck.", Lance replied.

"You want to know what I think?" Josh said, "I think it's that liquid courage he's got in his hand. He finally had the guts to ask you out."

"Well, it doesn't matter how it happened as long as it happened." Lance quipped.

"I can't argue with that," Josh said, still smiling. "Just do me a favor you two, go easy on the beer. You guys are important to me, and I don't want you to get hurt. Why don't you let me take you home later?"

Lance said, "We'll see".

"Fair enough," Josh said.

Lance asked, "Where's the bike?"

Josh said, "I figured I'd bring the pickup in case someone needed a ride home after drinking themselves into oblivion."

"Good idea," Lance said.

Becky looked back at the party and said, "Oh, Shit. Look, Cole and Lisa are fighting."

Josh quickly turned his head and saw Lisa and Cole in a heated discussion. He couldn't make out what they were saying but their body language said it wasn't pleasant. Becky ran over to where Cole and Lisa were and placed herself between them. She was screaming something at Cole and was able to get Lisa away from him. She and Lisa made their way to where Josh and Lance were waiting. As they approached them, Josh could hear Lisa saying that Cole had just broken up with her. She said, "That son-of-a-bitch used me for two years and then dumped me when he was getting ready to leave and go to college. He's a fucking asshole."

Becky had her arm around her friend, consoling her as they approached the pickup. Lisa was crying. It broke Josh's heart to see her hurting. Lance looked at Josh and saw the anger in his eyes. "Easy, Dude. Let it go." Lance said.

Josh said, "I'm not going to do anything...yet." Josh was glaring at Cole who was now laughing and carrying on with his football crew. They were all drunk and being more stupid than usual. He said to Lisa, "I'm sorry, Lis."

She said, "You warned me a year ago and I didn't listen. I should have broken up with his dumbass back then."

Josh said, "I know it hurts right now but you're going to be ok."

"You're damn right I am", Lisa said. "I'm better off."

Josh glanced back over to Cole and his boys and noticed the four of them coming their way. He hopped off the tailgate and closed it. Josh said, "They're coming over here. Don't turn around yet. When I tell you, step to your left a couple of steps. Lance, you and Becky stay where you are"

When Cole and his crew got about eight feet away Josh told Lisa to step aside.

"What do you want, Jensen?" Josh said.

"I want a piece of your ass, Bailey.", Cole replied.

Lisa, ignoring what Josh instructed her to do, placed

herself between Cole and Josh facing Cole she shouted, "Leave us alone, asshole."

"Out of my way, bitch", Cole yelled and slapped Lisa hard across her beautiful face and she fell to the ground.

"You just made a big mistake, Shithead.", Josh said.

Cole handed his beer to one of his posses and said, "You're next, asshole", and came at Josh swinging with his left hand. Josh knew he was a lefty by watching all those football games, so he was ready for it. Josh turned sideways and grabbed Cole's swinging arm and using his own momentum against him, shoved him aside. Cole lost his balance, tripped over his own feet, went face-first into the pickup's tailgate, and fell to the ground. Cole, sitting on the ground looked up at his crew and said, "Get that motherfucker." The three of them looked at each other and shook their heads collectively. One of them said, "You shouldn't have slapped Lisa, Dude. That wasn't cool. You're on your own." The three of them turned their backs on Cole and walked away.

"Well, it seems you're all alone, dipshit," Josh said. "Take my advice. Get up and take your drunk ass home."

"I'm not done with you, Bailey. Just give me a second to stand up."

Josh shook his head in dismay and said, "Look, you're done. If you try to come at me again, your nose won't be the only part of you in pain."

Cole slowly stood up and staggering tried punching Josh again, which Josh was easily able to avoid. With no hesitation, Josh punched Jacob square in his nose three times, bap, bap, bap, and then quickly punched him in the throat. Gagging, and trying to catch his breath, Cole fell to the ground again.

Josh's attention then went to Lisa who was still on the ground with Becky comforting her. "Are you alright," he asked Lisa.

"Yeah", she responded.

Josh asked Lance to help Becky get Lisa on her feet and returned his attention back to Cole who was groaning on the ground. Josh said to him, "You brought all this on yourself. Now look at you, Mr. star quarterback. You're a good football player, Jensen. Don't waste your future being stupid and starting trouble. Get up and go home."

Lisa now standing said, "Wait a second." She walked to Cole and said, "Look at me."

Cole stupidly looked up at her and Lisa spit directly into his eye. "You piece of shit." She spoke.

The onlookers who had gathered around laughed loudly at Cole and slowly began to scatter.

Josh was pleasantly surprised to see Lisa in this new light. He had never seen her angry before. Cole got up to his feet silently and with his head down walked to his car, got in, and drove away.

Josh looked at Lance and said, "Do you remember what I told you last year?"

"I remember. You didn't lie." Lance said.

Lisa lunged at Josh and wrapped her arms around him. She said, "Thanks, Josh. You're my hero."

CHAPTER 8

Few things are better to wake up to than the smell of freshly cooked bacon. Josh got himself dressed and went downstairs to find Aunt Lo and Uncle Woody sitting at the breakfast table eating. They passed on the usual morning greetings and Josh went about filling his plate with scrambled eggs, hash browns, and that awesome bacon. He sat down and began eating while Uncle Woody and Aunt Lo watched him shove food in his mouth at a rapid pace.

After a moment Woody said, "I got a call from Dan Fisher this morning."

Josh paused his fast chewing to look at Woody. He said, "So I guess Lisa told him what happened last night. Is he mad?"

"Not at all," Woody said. "In fact, he was glad you stuck up for her. He said you got Cole Jensen pretty good."

"I guess. He slapped her and I had to do something. He threw two punches at me and missed both times. I only hit him four times. I don't think I'll ever understand why some people can't handle their beer and get violent."

"Were you drinking?" Lo asked.

"Of course not," Josh responded. "I don't like it." He continued, "Did he say if Lisa is alright?'

"She's fine. She told Dan that you were her hero." Woody said.

"She did?" he said.

Aunt Lo said, "I think you should call her and ask her out."

"I don't think she's ready for that," Josh replied. "I want to, but she just broke up with Cole and I think she probably wants some time to herself for a while."

Lo looked at Woody as if to say, 'Your turn.'

"We happen to know that she wants you to ask her out. So, our recommendation is for you to do that very thing." Woody announced. "It's not as if you two don't know each other, you've been friends for a long time, for heaven's sake. You know each other well. What are you afraid of?"

"Hurting her," Josh said solemnly.

Lo looked at Josh with a surprised look on her face. She said, "What makes you think you'll hurt her?"

"I don't want to be like all those guys who came around wanting my mom."

"Oh, Honey," Lo said, "You will never be like any of those guys. You are a kind, generous, and caring young man. We all know how you feel about her and it is not in your nature to ever hurt her."

"I don't know," Josh said, "I'll think about it."

Woody chimed in, "Well don't take too long. Remember what I told you about having one shot? If you wait too long, it'll be too late. You must take chances, Josh. Otherwise, you'll regret not taking them. Call her. Call Lisa. Today. Make a date for tonight. Take her to the movies or something."

"Fine," Josh relented.

"And dress up nice," Lo said. "No t-shirt. Wear a button-down shirt and your best jeans. Girls like it when their dates dress nicely. It shows you care."

"Take the pickup too. Save the bike for next time." Woody said.

"You two aren't going to let this go, are you?" Josh quipped.

Lo and Woody laughed, and Lo said emphatically, "No, we are not."

* * *

Dan and Nancy Fisher were the proud parents of Lisa and Lori Fisher. They owned and operated Fisher's Farm Store in town and were known to be fair and generous business owners. There were many times when Dan would offer credit to struggling farmers as well as to other business owners. The Fisher family was well-known and well-liked in Anthony.

Dan had a bald head and wore a mustache. He was average in height and weight. Not unattractive but not incredibly handsome either. He was a voracious reader and took exceptionally loving care of his family. He doted on his two daughters and he and Nancy raised the girls to be kind, considerate young ladies.

Nancy was a woman of generosity like her husband, Dan. She had long, blonde hair and kept herself in pristine condition never allowing anyone to see her without makeup on. She passed this trait along to her two daughters and encouraged both to stand out among their peers at school. Whether it was through athletics, cheerleading, or exceptional grades, she wanted her daughters to be well above average at whatever they were interested in. She did not force any activity on them, she allowed them to decide for themselves what path they chose. Once chosen, though, Nancy would be hands-on with guidance for both of her daughters.

Lori Fisher was two years younger than Lisa. They both had blonde hair like their mother and to see both together it was easy to tell that they were sisters. Growing up they had the same arguments any siblings might have but as they grew, they became more friendly toward each other. While Lisa was interested in cheerleading, Lori was an avid basketball player, and she also ran track. The 100-yard hurdles were her specialty.

The day after the incident at the lake, the family was seated at the kitchen table having breakfast. It was a Saturday morning and Dan would be going to their store soon to open for the day. Lori had no plans other than to be lazy and maybe shoot some hoops in their driveway later. Dan had risen earlier and called Woody Bailey. He wanted to thank Josh for what he had done for Lisa the night before. She had told him the whole story about the break-up and the so-called fight between Cole and Josh. Dan said, "I'm sorry you're sad about the break-up but to tell you the truth, I never trusted that kid anyway."

"I know," Lisa responded. "And I'm not sad."

"Can I make a suggestion?" he asked her. "Why don't you date Josh? He is a good kid, and it's obvious that he would do anything to protect you."

"If he asked me out, I'd go." Lisa said, "In all these years he's never insinuated that he liked me in that way. We've been friends since he moved here, and we talk a lot, but I don't think he's interested in dating me."

The entire table erupted with laughter at Lisa's assessment. They all knew that Josh had had a crush on her for years. Apparently, the only one who did not know was Lisa. Lisa said, "What's everyone laughing about?"

Lori spoke and said, "He's liked you since you were in seventh grade. It's funny that you don't know that."

Dan said, "What's even more amazing is that he hasn't asked you out before. That's a mystery. I like a good mystery and I'm going to solve this one."

"I really had no idea he felt like you say. He's always treated me like a buddy." Lisa said. "If he had asked me out a long time ago, I never would have wasted two years with Cole."

Nancy spoke, "You need to tell him that when you see him."

An hour later the telephone rang at the Fisher residence. That phone call would change Lisa's life forever...in a good way.

* * *

Josh came bounding down the stairs excitedly. He was dressed in his finest blue button-down shirt and his newest

Levis. Uncle Woody and Aunt Lo were watching the news on TV. Something about Iran-Contra. Josh didn't care. His appearance in the Bailey living room made Uncle Woody and Aunt Lo turn their heads to look at him. Aunt Lo said, "Well don't you look handsome?"

"Thanks," Josh replied. "I'm a nervous wreck."

Woody shook his head and said, "Relax. You're going to be fine. You two are overdue for this."

"I guess we'll find out," Josh said.

Woody said, "Just remember to be a gentleman. Open the truck door for her. Be considerate and be funny."

Josh said, "We're going to see an Eddie Murphy movie, he can take care of the funny part."

"But he's not dating Lisa, you are," Woody replied.

"Good point," Josh said. "Wish me luck."

Aunt Lo said, "You don't need luck. Just be who you are."

Woody said, "Yeah, what Lo said."

Josh walked out the back door and into the shop climbed into the pick-up, started the engine, and drove toward town.

Woody turned to Lo and asked, "What do you think?"

She said, "It reminds me of us."

"How so?" Woody asked.

"You were nervous on our first date too, remember?"

"No, I wasn't. I just wanted you to think I was nervous so you would do most of the talking."

"Liar," she said.

* * *

Josh parked in front of the Fisher home, took a deep breath, and said to himself, "Here goes nothing." and exited the truck. He had been to their home several times over the years when he was younger for Lisa's birthday parties that Nancy would host. The last time was for Lisa's fourteenth birthday three years ago. She and Josh were now seventeen and were preparing for their senior and final year of high school. The Fisher home was a two-story white house with a large porch. The lawn was well-manicured, and Josh knew that Dan Fisher took pride in his upkeep of the front yard. There was a garage with a basketball hoop attached to it where Lori would practice shooting. He walked up the stairs to the front door and rang the doorbell. He heard someone coming to the door and hoped that it was Lisa. When the door opened, he was greeted by both Nancy and Dan. "Come on in, Josh," Nancy said. "It's good to see you."

The house was kept in pristine cleanliness. There would be nothing out of place and Nancy made sure of that. They led him to Dan's den where there was a desk with two chairs facing it. Dan told Josh to have a seat while he sat in his office chair. The walls were covered with shelves of books which Josh had always admired. Nancy took the chair next to Josh. Josh said, "I've always admired your book collection, Mr. Fisher. It's quite a library."

Dan said, "I hear you're a big reader."

Josh answered, "There are few things I enjoy more, Sir."

Dan looked at Nancy smiling, and Nancy said, "Josh, we just wanted to thank you for sticking up for Lisa last night. We want you to know how grateful we are."

Josh said, "It was nothing. I couldn't let Cole get away with treating her like he did. Slapping her and calling her vile names. I'm glad I was there to help."

Just then Josh heard someone rumbling down the stairs next to the den. He peered over and caught Lori peeking in the room. Josh said, "Hey, Lori. How ya doing?"

"Hey, Josh," Lori said grinning. "I'm good. It's about time you asked her out." She laughed and ran back up the stairs yelling "Lisa, your hero is here."

Nancy and Dan chuckled while Josh smiled and rolled his eyes. "I've often wondered what it would be like to have a brother or sister. Now I have a good idea.," he said.

Nancy said, "They can be a handful, but we wouldn't trade having them for anything in the world."

Dan asked, "How are Woody and Lo?"

Josh replied, "They're good. Pestering me about all this all day. Telling me what to wear and how to act. I know they mean well, though."

They chatted a bit more about their store and about harvest coming up soon. After a few minutes, Lisa appeared. She was wearing denim shorts and a loose-fitting white blouse. Her blonde hair was perfect. "Hey, Mr. Hero," she said.

Josh smiled and said, "Hey, Ms. Instigator."

They all laughed, and Lisa said, "Are you ready to go?"

"I am," Josh said and rose from his seat. He said to Dan and Nancy "I appreciate your hospitality. Rest assured I'll have her home at a decent hour."

Dan said, "We know you will. You two have a good time."

Nancy said, "Thanks, again, Josh."

"You're welcome, Ma'am."

Josh and Lisa walked out the front door and toward the pick-up. Lisa asked, "What was my mom thanking you for?"

He said, "For sticking up for you last night, I guess."

"Oh, how embarrassing". Lisa said.

"Not at all," Josh replied.

As they got close to the truck Lisa asked," Where's the bike? You know you owe me a ride, remember?"

"I do but I figured that since this is our first date, I would bring the truck so I could do this." He immediately opened the passenger side door of the pick-up to allow Lisa easier access.

Lisa smiled and said, "Very clever."

"Thanks, but to be honest, it was Uncle Woody's suggestion. I can't take credit for it. I wish I could." Josh said.

✶ ✶ ✶

The Anthony movie theater was constructed in the late 1930s. It had undergone many renovations over the decades. Some believed that the first movie shown there was 'The Wizard of Oz.' It had a classic look of old-time theaters with red, blue, and green neon lights on the marquee. The letters showing which movie was currently playing were in perfect arrangement. On this occasion it read, 'Now Showing-Beverly Hills Cop II.'

Josh parked the pick-up down the street, got out, and ran around the front of the truck so he could open the door for Lisa. She climbed out and they began the 200-foot walk to the theater on the main street. Lisa reached down and interlocked her fingers with Josh's, as they strolled down the sidewalk.

Josh's heart was beating fast as this action was not expected. As they approached the theater Josh noticed Lance and Becky waiting in line to get their tickets for the movie. Lance turned and noticed Josh and Lisa holding hands, he nudged Becky, and she turned around to see. Both were smiling big at what they were witnessing. The foursome greeted each other warmly. Lance leaned over to Josh and said, "It's about time."

Josh said, "You're the second person to say that to me tonight."

They got their tickets and went inside making a direct line to the concession stand. The aroma of freshly popped popcorn filled the lobby. Josh purchased a bucket of popcorn a Dr. Pepper for Lisa and a Coke for himself. It was decided that the four of them would sit together and they made their way down the aisle. The seats had recently been replaced and had the look of old-style theater seats only more comfortable. Red velvet covered the cushions, and the armrests were small. They sat and watched the movie. Laughing at Eddie Murphy's antics. When Lisa wasn't drinking from her cup, her hand stayed interlocked with Josh's. Josh found it difficult to concentrate on the movie. He was finally on a date with Lisa, the girl of his dreams. Dreams that had been with him for five years. Occasionally, Lisa would glance at him and smile at seeing Josh smiling and thinking he was enjoying the movie. Josh was not smiling at the movie. He was smiling for a different reason.

When the movie ended, they all walked out, said their goodbyes, and made their way toward their vehicles. Josh and Lisa, hand-in-hand, made their way slowly to the pick-up. Josh opened the door for her again, got in on the driver's side, and said, "It's still early. Any thoughts?"

Lisa said, "Can we go somewhere and talk for a while?"

Josh said, "Sure. Lake?"

Lisa nodded and said, "Yeah."

They drove the short four-mile ride to the lake and found a place where they could talk in private. It was a warm evening and there was not a cloud in the sky. The moon was glowing brightly, and the glow reflected on the water. Josh looked up and noticed the many stars that were visible.

"Do you feel like walking?" Lisa asked.

Josh said, "Sure. Whatever you want. Your wish is my command."

Lisa smiled and said, "Why thank you, my hero."

They got out of the truck and made their way along the shore of the lake. Josh would occasionally pick up a rock and throw it into the water. They talked a little about the movie and their plans for the summer. Finally, they reached a park bench where they could sit and look out at the water. They sat and Josh fixed his gaze on the stars above while Lisa looked at him. She said, "Can I ask you something?"

Josh said, "Sure, you can ask me anything."

"Why did you take so long to ask me out?" she asked.

Josh thought for a moment and replied, "I honestly didn't think you would accept."

"What made you think that?"

"Well," Josh said. "You're so popular at school and I'm somewhat of an outcast, a nerd, a nobody."

"First of all," Lisa responded. "You're not an outcast or any of those things. As far as me being popular goes, that's all an illusion. There's nothing real about it."

"What do you mean?" Josh questioned. "Everyone likes you. You're friendly with everyone. I don't understand."

"That's not what I mean. I know everyone likes me but that is the illusion itself. Once we graduate, the popularity you think I have will end instantly the moment we get our diplomas" She continued, "Most of the girls I hang out with, other than Becky, use me as sort of a status symbol. They want to hang out with me because they think that doing so will make them popular. Maybe it does, and maybe it doesn't. I don't know. What I do know is that when school ends, so will my so-called popularity."

"I had no idea you felt like this. You always seem so happy.", Josh said.

Lisa said, "I'm thinking about quitting cheerleading."

Josh said, "Why? You're so good at it?"

"I don't know," she said.

"I support whatever you want to do but I have to say that I really love watching you do all those cheers and the gymnastics that you do with it," Josh said.

"Thanks," Lisa said. "I know you like watching me. I've seen you." She giggled.

"What can I say?" Josh said. "You're absolutely gorgeous and it is very hard for me to not watch you."

"You are too sweet," Lisa said. "I'll probably keep doing it since this will be our last year."

"I, for one, appreciate that," Josh said.

Lisa thought for a moment and said, "Can I ask you something else? It's something I've wondered about for a long time."

"Yes?" Josh said,

"When you first moved here, you said your mom died and so you came to live with Woody and Lo."

Josh hesitated and said, "Yeah."

"My family has known Woody and Lo for a long time. Long before you came here. Why didn't they ever talk about you and your mom?"

Josh turned his head and looked up at the stars filling the sky. He said trying to change the subject, "There sure are a lot of stars out tonight."

Lisa lightly touched Josh's' cheek and turned his head gently to face her. "Josh," she said. "What happened to your mom?"

Josh turned his head again and looked out at the moon glow on the lake. He took a deep breath and said, "What I'm about to tell you must stay with you. You can never tell anyone. Not even your folks." He continued, "The only people who know this story, that live here anyway, are me, Uncle Woody and Aunt Lo. The only reason I'm telling you is because you asked, and I won't lie to you about anything ever."

Lisa looked at him with a puzzled gaze. She said, "I swear, I won't tell anyone."

Josh kept his eyes focused on the water, sighed, and started the story. "When I was twelve years old, my mom came home late at night with a guy. They had been drinking."

He told her about everything that happened that night. The bat to Bruce's face and leg. His mother was pistol-whipped. Him shooting Bruce. Then he stopped talking. Lisa could tell it was difficult for Josh to be reminded of what happened. Josh looked down at the ground and spoke. "I watched her die; I couldn't help her."

Lisa began to cry seeing the pain wash over Josh's face. She could sense the guilt that he felt about not being able to save his mom. At that moment, she felt guilty for asking Josh about her. "Oh my god, Josh." Lisa said sadly, "How horrible for you. I'm sorry I pressured you to tell me."

Josh shook his head and said, "It's ok. You were going to find out someday. It might as well be now."

Lisa grabbed Josh's hand and said, "I promise not to tell anyone. How did you come to live with Woody and Lo?"

"They read my mom's obituary in the Eagle and came to get me. They didn't even know I existed until they saw Mom's obituary."

Then Lisa reached up again and placed her hands on both sides of Josh's face, turning him to face her. She raised her face to his and lightly kissed him on his lips. This was not out of passion or lust. It was out of genuine concern. "I'm so sorry you had to go through all that. I had no idea."

Josh nodded grimly, "Yeah, it was bad. The worst thing ever. Uncle Woody and Aunt Loanne saved my life. They rescued me. There's no telling how my life would have gone without them coming to my rescue. It most likely wouldn't have been pleasant. I'm very lucky to have them. So, you don't think less of me?"

Lisa said, "Of course not. Why would you ask me that?"

"I took a life. Doesn't that bother you?"

Lisa looked at him adoringly and said, "You had to do what you had to do in that moment. I think you really are a hero. You were then and you are now." She continued, "Now I understand."

Josh asked, "You understand what?"

"Those times when you helped others against bullies. It all makes sense to me now," she said. "You never backed down from Cole when everyone else did. It's like you have no fear."

"I do hate bullies, that's for sure and I do have one major fear." He said, "Hurting you. That's the only thing I'm afraid of. That's one reason why it took me so long to ask you out. I do not want to hurt you ever and I never would. That's why I don't drink. Because I've seen what it can do to some people. It changes them."

Lisa nodded her head and said, "I understand. Honestly, I don't think you would ever hurt me. You're my protector, my hero."

They both stood and hugged each other. Lisa kissed him again. He could smell the intoxicating aroma of her hair. Apple, he believed, and the vanilla perfume she was wearing made him weak. They held their embrace for a long moment then made their way back to the pickup. They drove back to town and pulled up in front of Lisa's home. They got out of the truck and Josh walked her to the door. He said, "Thank you for an excellent evening. I'm sorry I got so emotional talking about my mom. I'm very embarrassed."

Lisa said, "It's ok. I understand a lot more about you now. You're a great guy, Josh. I'm glad you finally called me. When do I get that motorcycle ride?"

Josh smiled and said, "How about tomorrow?"

Lisa responded with her own smile and said, "Perfect. I can't wait."

They kissed again and Lisa entered the house. Josh walked to the truck, got in, and drove home smiling the entire way.

* * *

"How'd it go?" Uncle Woody asked Josh the next morning.

"Perfect," Josh said. "I may have made a mistake, though. I told her about Mom."

"I see." Woody said, "What makes you think it was a mistake?"

"I don't know. I just feel funny about it. I asked her not to tell anyone and she promised she wouldn't."

"If Lisa Fisher promised she wouldn't tell your story to anyone, then you can believe her," Woody said. "What's your plan for today? Are you going to see her?"

"I promised her a ride on the bike a long time ago. I told her back then that I'd give her a ride the minute she broke up with Cole. So that's what we're going to do."

"Okay, well, take Lo's helmet with you so she'll have one to use." Woody insisted.

"Will do," Josh said.

Josh walked down to the shop and grabbed Lo's helmet and strapped it to his sissy bar. He fired up the engine and revved the throttle a couple of times. The thunderous exhaust echoed throughout the shop. He climbed on and rode to town to pick up his new girlfriend.

* * *

Lisa could hear Josh coming up their street. She judged him to be about two blocks away. Then she excitedly ran to the kitchen where the rest of the family was and announced that Josh was here, and she would be home later.

"I want a ride," Lori exclaimed.

"I'm sure Josh will give you a ride someday but today he's all mine," Lisa said.

Josh parked the bike in front of the house, turned off the engine, and climbed off.

He looked up and saw Lisa running toward him. She looked fantastic. She was wearing tight jeans and a tight, black shirt with spaghetti straps. She was in low-cut boots, and she had sunglasses on. Her gorgeous blonde hair was braided in the back. And of course, her make-up was perfectly placed. Josh smiled as she hugged him tightly and gave him a small kiss. She said, "Where are we going, Hero?"

Josh said, "Wherever you want. You're the queen and I am merely your jester with a Harley."

"Let's go by Becky's house first. I want her and Lance to see me on your bike." She exclaimed.

"Is he at her house?" Josh asked.

"Yep. They're just hanging out. Lance took his guitar over there. She likes watching him play." She said.

"Okay," Josh said, "You, my lady, are the first to ever ride with me on my mechanical steed. That means a couple of things. First, try to relax and go with the flow. Don't get tensed up. Second, please do not wave your arms all around or wiggle. Third, by riding with me, you hereby agree to allow my left hand to rub, squeeze, or pat your left leg while riding. Do you agree with these terms as I have presented them to you?"

Lisa laughed and said, "I do hereby agree, kind sir."

Josh straddled the bike and started the engine. Then he instructed Lisa on the best way to climb on. "It's like getting on a horse." He spoke. "Left foot on the peg, bring your right leg across the seat and you're on." She did as he instructed and Josh said, "Are you ready?"

Lisa could not stop smiling and she said, "Let 'er rip."

Josh placed the bike in gear, revved the engine a couple of times, and slowly released the clutch lever. As they pulled away from the curb, Lisa reached around Josh's waist with both hands and held on tightly. Josh reached down with his left hand a gave Lisa's leg an assuring 'love tap.' It was another dream fulfilled for Joshua Bailey.

CHAPTER 9

Emily Baker, 20, was the only child of Douglas and Rebecca Baker. Her parents had told her when she was younger that she did have an older brother who sadly died when he was an infant. The Bakers operated a steakhouse and bar in St. Joseph, Missouri. Growing up and throughout high school, Emily, or 'Em' as she preferred to be called, was a good student. She was an avid reader, and she participated in sports. Volleyball was her favorite and she had the right body for it. Tall and skinny, she could out-leap almost anyone. She had long brown hair that she would tie back when she played volleyball. After graduating high school, she and her best friend, Jessica Brown got an apartment together in St. Joe. The two had been best friends their entire lives. They never kept secrets from each other, and each was always there for the other when needed. Em worked for her parents at the steakhouse and bar that they owned. She waited tables at first then hostess and eventually learned the books. In another year she would be legal to bartend.

The steakhouse was immensely popular and had been in business for many years. Rarely a complaint from customers and when there was a complaint, it was unfounded. On weekends, when the dinner crowd dispersed, the bar would become lively. There were bands that played on Friday and Saturday nights. Sometimes rock bands and other times country bands. Douglas did an excellent job booking bands for the bar and Em learned a lot about the business of booking them herself. Douglas and Rebecca made no secret of the fact that Em would someday own and operate the steakhouse when they retired.

On those many weekend nights, a local man named Derek Johnson would appear at the bar. He was a heavy drinker, and rumor had it that he was also a cocaine dealer. No one knew for sure if it was true, but it was a well-known assumption. Nearly every night, if Emily was there, Derek would make passes at her attempting to date her and each time, Em would turn him down. She would let him know that she was not interested in him but appreciated the offer and thanked him for continuing to patronize the bar. Derek was relentless in his pursuit of Emily Baker.

Only two weeks before, Douglas Baker was closing the bar late at night and was about to lock the doors when two men wearing masks shoved their way inside. Douglas ran to his office and grabbed his .38 pistol. He stayed behind his desk, gun raised and ready to fire. Suddenly one of the men kicked the door to the office open and Douglas fired a shot hitting the bandit in the chest. The other man heard the shot and came running, peeked around the corner of the bar, and saw his partner lying in a pool of blood. "You son-of-a-bitch. You shot my brother." He yelled.

With his adrenalin pumping the robber began firing round after round from his semi-automatic rifle toward the office. Two of the bullets hit Douglas. One in the chest and the other in his head.

He was killed instantly. The shooter looked around to grab all the cash he could find, ran out the back door, and fled.

Two days later, the bandit was caught and arrested. His trial was pending.

One week after the funeral for Douglas Baker, Emily was in her father's office looking through files when she came across a large manilla envelope. Written on it was only her name, 'Emily.' With a puzzled look on her face, she opened the envelope and removed the contents. What she found inside would shake up her world as she knew it. Her life would never quite be the same.

Emily placed the contents back into the envelope, grabbed her purse and keys, and ran out of the bar to her waiting green Camaro. She raced to her mother's home, ran inside, and found her mother sitting silently in her favorite chair in their living room. Emily walked up to her mother, slammed the envelope onto the coffee table, and shouted. "You want to explain this to me?"

Rebecca looked at the envelope and her face turned white with fear and trepidation. She looked back up at Emily and said, "I've been waiting for this moment for twenty years. It's time you learned the truth."

Emily snapped back saying, "You mean the part about me being adopted? I want the whole story. Right now."

Rebecca said, "Sit down, Em. There's much to tell you." She continued. "Yes, your father and I adopted you right after you were born."

"I can read," said Emily. "I want details. For starters, tell me who Angel Katherine Bailey is. Is she my real mother?"

Rebecca nodded and said, "Yes"

"And what about my father? The birth certificate says father unknown" Emily asked.

"I'm not sure," Rebecca replied.

"Why didn't you and Dad tell me? I'm twenty years old. I'm sure I would have rather found out from you two than to find this shit in his office."

"We should have," Rebecca admitted. "I'm sorry you found out this way."

"I want to know everything. You owe me that." Emily demanded.

Rebecca sighed and began telling the story.

"When your mother was seventeen years old, she and this guy, I don't remember his name, I think it started with a 'B', Bill or Bruce or something. Anyway, they moved to Pleasanton, Kansas. At the time, we owned a small café there and Angel was pregnant with you. We hired her as a server and took her in. Not long after they arrived, the guy she came there with left without a word. Angel was stranded with little money and no place to go. We invited her to stay with us until she could get her life together. In the meantime, we had already made plans to buy the steakhouse and move here."

Emily looked horrified as Rebecca continued the story.

"She, Angel, decided it would be best for you if she put you up for adoption. She wanted you to have a better life than she could give you. So, your father and I agreed to adopt you and raise you as our own."

Emily was stone-faced upon hearing the story. She said, "Where is she now?"

"I honestly don't know. We moved here and brought you with us right after you were born." Rebecca said. "We haven't heard from her since that day."

"How could she just give me up like that?" Emily said with tears coming down her face. "I don't understand."

Rebecca said, "I understand how you feel but try to put yourself in her place. She had no money. From what she told us, her father, your grandfather, kicked her out of his house when she got pregnant. She was with this guy, and he took her to Pleasanton and dumped her off there. This was in 1967, Emily. Things were crazy back then. Teenagers all over the country were doing all kinds of drugs. LSD, marijuana, etcetera. Angel was part of all of it. The drugs, the sex. It was so bad that we thought for sure you wouldn't survive. But when you were born, we were so thankful that you were healthy. We were pleasantly surprised that you were."

Emily sat motionless taking in all this new information.

Rebecca said. "We tried extremely hard to bring you up in

a loving home. Your father and I were determined to give you as good a life as we could. I am so sorry we didn't tell you sooner."

Emily was silent for a moment then she said, "I appreciate everything you and Daddy have done for me. Knowing what I know now, my life could have been much worse. I'm thankful for you and Dad."

Rebecca began to cry. She had been worried about this moment for a long time and now a sense of relief came over her like a tidal wave. They hugged for a long moment. Then Emily said, "I want to find her."

Rebecca said, "I understand. I'll help any way I can."

"I don't know where to start," Emily said.

"Go to Pleasanton, Kansas, and ask around. I would start with the sheriff's department and work from there. Maybe they'll know where to find her."

Emily looked down at the envelope with the adoption papers and her original birth certificate inside. She pulled out the certificate and looked at it again.

Name of child: Emily Kay Bailey
Name of mother: Angel Katherine Bailey
Name of father: Unknown
Date of birth: July 1st, 1968

* * *

Emily drove home and found Jessica watching television. She said, "I was adopted."

Jessica asked, "What? What do you mean you were adopted?"

Emily explained the envelope and the confrontation she had with her mother. She said, "I'm going to go to Pleasanton, Kansas, and find her. You want to go?"

Jessica responded, "Hell, yeah. When do we leave?"

* * *

The next morning, Emily and Jessica packed enough clothing to last them a few days and loaded the suitcases into Emily's Camaro and they left St. Joseph.

"How are we going to find her?" Jessica asked.

"I guess we'll start at the Sheriff's office and see if they know anything. I called them but they wouldn't give me any information over the phone. It's just as well, I'd rather just go there and find her in person." Em replied.

They made the two-hour drive to Pleasanton with no delays. Even going around Kansas City was a breeze surprisingly, especially on a Monday. When they arrived in Pleasanton, they stopped at a convenience store and asked the store clerk where the sheriff's office was. The clerk gave Emily directions, and they found the building with no problem. Emily parked the car, took a deep breath, exhaled, and said, "What do I say when I find her?" She asked Jessica.

"Just tell her who you are and go from there."

They climbed out of the car walked up the steps to the station and walked inside. Emily was carrying the manilla envelope. They noticed a lady sitting behind a counter looking busy with paperwork. The lady asked, "What can I do for you ladies?"

Emily said, "We're looking for an Angel Bailey."

The lady said, "Oh? Um, wait here." Then she stood and walked down a hallway. After a moment she came back and said that Sheriff Hilts would be right out and for them to have a seat. Em and Jessica took seats on the bench across from the receptionist's desk. A few seconds later a man dressed in his uniform appeared. He looked to be in his early 30's, smartly dressed in his uniform. He was tall and clean-shaven. "Good morning, ladies. I'm Sheriff Holts. Come on back to my office."

They followed the Sheriff down the hallway, and he led them to what appeared to be his office. It had an old desk with two chairs facing it. There were plaques and framed photographs hanging on the walls. He told the ladies to have a seat, which they did.

"Phyllis tells me you're looking for Angel Bailey." He spoke.

Emily said, "Yes."

"Can I ask why?" he questioned.

Emily said, "She's my mother. She put me up for adoption when I was born and I just recently found out about her." She opened the manilla envelope that had been her focus for the past two days, she reached in and pulled out her birth certificate and the adoption papers. All of which she handed to the sheriff. Sheriff Holts looked at them and then looked back at Emily with a sullen look on his face.

"If you know where she is, I would appreciate you telling me where I can find her," Emily said.

Sheriff Holts sighed heavily and said, "I'm terribly sorry to have to tell you this but Angel died seven years ago."

A look of shock and bewilderment came over Emily's face. She said, "How?"

"She was murdered." He spoke.

"How? Why? I want to know what happened." Emily said.

"Alright, you deserve to know so I'll tell you." He continued. "Seven years ago, I was new on the job. One late night I received a report of a domestic dispute at a mobile home park just outside town. It was called the Blue View Mobile Home Park. It closed a year or so ago. Now it's just a vacant lot. We had received calls from there a few times before, but this time was different. Very different. I'll never forget what I saw when I got there. It haunts me to this day. I won't go into the details but what I found when I arrived, I saw Josh Bailey sitting on his front porch. He was twelve or thirteen then"

"Wait," Emily said. "Who's Josh Bailey?"

"Angel's son. You mean to tell me that you don't know about Josh?" He asked.

Emily was getting agitated. "I told you that I just found out I was adopted. The only reason I know Angel's name is because of my birth certificate. Are you high or just stupid?"

Jessica said, "Easy, Em. He's just trying to help."

"Then he needs to do better," Emily said.

"You sound like Josh the day after your mom's passing. You have the same anger he had. Please, I apologize. It's been seven years since I've had that night on my mind. I'll try to explain the best I know how. It was only Josh and Angel living in their mobile home. How old are you if I may ask?"

Emily said, "I'm 20."

Sheriff Holts nodded his head and said, "Then you must be Josh's older sister."

"I can't believe this," Emily exclaimed. "In 24 hours, I've learned I was adopted, my birth mother was murdered, and I have a brother who's two years younger than me."

"Holy shit," Jessica said. "I'm so sorry, Em."

Sheriff Holts said, "Yeah. Me too. I can't imagine what you're going through right now. Honestly, I didn't know Angel had a daughter until this very moment."

"Where is my brother?" She asked.

"The last I heard he was picked up by a couple of relatives who had a farm in south central Kansas. After your mom's death, he was staying with a pastor here in town. His name is Raymond Stevens. He's retired now but still lives here. I can give him a call if you like."

"Please. I'd like to talk to him." Emily said.

"In a moment, but first there's something you should know. The night your mother was killed, Josh, your brother, shot and killed the man who assaulted and murdered your mother." He continued. "He admitted it. He also beat the man severely with a baseball bat. All the evidence we collected supported his story. He was not charged with a crime. The County attorney wouldn't press charges since it was ruled self-defense. The exact cause of your mother's death was blunt force trauma. The man who killed her pistol-whipped her." He said, "I'm so sorry to have to tell you this but you have the right to know."

"You say my brother was twelve or thirteen at the time?" Emily asked.

"As I recall, yes". Holts said.

They sat in silence for a moment then Jessica asked, "Where is Angel buried?"

"She's buried at Pleasanton cemetery. I can take you out there if you'd like"

Jessica looked at Emily who was still trying to take in all this information. She said, "What do think, Em? Should we?"

Emily nodded her head 'yes'.

"I'll call pastor Stevens and let him know you'll be stopping by. I'll take you there after the cemetery" Holts said.

* * *

They followed Sheriff Holts through town and pulled into the cemetery. Jessica was driving. Emily sat silent the entire way. They turned into the cemetery and Sheriff Holts got out of his cruiser and the ladies exited the Camaro. Holts walked back to them and said, "This way."

Em and Jessica followed Holts across several plots until they arrived at Angel's final resting place. They looked down and Emily reading the small, flat marker out loud said "Angel Katherine Bailey. Born June 5th, 1950. Died August 21st, 1982. She was only thirty-two years old." She looked at Jessica and said, "I was fourteen when she died, and I had no idea."

On the way to Pastor Stevens' house, Emily said, "Let's try to get this straight. My birth mother was born in 1950, she got kicked out of her parents, grandparents' home, when she was seventeen. That was in 1967. I was born in 1968 and was adopted by Douglas and Rebecca Baker to raise me. In the meantime, my birth mother gave birth to my brother two years after I was born. Twelve years later, my brother shoots and kills the man who murdered my mother." Emily took a deep breath. "Does that sound about right?"

Jessica said, "I think so."

"Makes me wonder what other surprises are waiting for me." Emily said, "You know what else is crazy? We only live two hours away from here."

They followed Sheriff Holts into town until he parked his car in front of a modest white house. He got out and walked back to their car as Emily and Jessica got out of the Camaro. He said, "This is where Pastor Stevens lives. As I mentioned earlier, he's retired now. Hopefully, he'll be able to give you more information about your mom and Josh."

The three of them walked up to the house and Holts rang the doorbell. Pastor Stevens opened the door and invited them inside. Sheriff Holts introduced them to each other and said, "I can't stay. I need to get back to the station." He turned to Emily and said, "Again, I'm so sorry about your mom. If there's anything I can do, just let me know."

Emily said, "Thanks. You've been very helpful."

Sheriff Holts walked down the steps of the porch, got into his cruiser, and drove off. Pastor Stevens invited the ladies into the house and led them to his living room where they all took seats. Emily and Jessica sat on the sofa and Pastor Stevens sat in an armchair across from them. He said, "Which one of you is Emily?"

Emily said, "Me. What can you tell me about my mother and my brother? Any information would be very helpful."

Pastor Stevens said. "I'll tell you everything I can remember. My memory is beginning to fail me. What did Sheriff Holts tell you so far?"

Emily told the pastor what Holts had told them earlier about Josh killing the man who killed their mother and that all of this was new information to her. She told him that she had been adopted by a nice couple when she was born, and they moved to St. Joseph shortly after the adoption. Plus, she had no idea that she had been adopted until yesterday nor did she know that she had a brother until today. Let alone that her mother had been murdered.

"That's a lot to take in, in a short amount of time." Pastor Stevens said. I knew your mom vaguely. Such a tragedy what happened to her and your brother. I had no idea that your mom had a daughter. You must have been born before I met her. She worked as a waitress at a small café here. That's really the only time I ever saw her. When my wife and I would eat there. I didn't know your brother until the night of the... incident."

"Can you tell me where my brother is?" Emily asked.

Pastor Stevens said, "A very nice couple came a couple of weeks after your mom's passing. They had paperwork proving that they were relatives of Josh. They went to court and gained custody of him and as far as I can remember, they took him to Anthony, Kansas, I think. They had a farm there they said."

"Do you remember their names?" Emily asked.

"I'm sure their name was Bailey. The man's name was Woody, and I think his wife's name was Loanna or Loanne. Something like that. That's the last thing I knew."

"Is there anything else you can think of?" Emily asked.

"I'm not a person who would ever condone violence. That night when your brother killed that man was horrific, to say the least. I believe he did what he had to do to protect himself and your mom the best way a twelve-year-old could." He said, "I wonder about him often. How is he doing? Is he having a good life? Seven years is a long time. You know, now that I look at you, there is a resemblance. You do look a lot like your mother. She was very pretty. Mixed up, but pretty."

"What was my brother like? I know you didn't know him very well but is there anything you can think of about him?" Emily asked.

"Well." Pastor Stevens said, "You must remember that his mother had just died, and Josh took the life of the person who took well... your mom's life. He was only twelve years old and that's a lot for a kid his age to have to deal with. He stayed here with us for a couple of weeks as I recall. He was very quiet, kept to himself, and didn't say much. What I remember the most about him was that he would read a lot. While most kids his age were watching TV, he was always reading."

Emily and Jessica rose and thanked pastor Stevens for his time. Pastor Stevens said he was glad to help. He said, "If you find Josh, give him my best and tell him I hope he's doing well. He was a good kid that got mixed up in a bad situation."

"We certainly will," Emily said. "Thanks again."

Emily and Jessica got back into the Camaro. They sat in silence for a moment, finally, Jessica said, "What now?"

Emily said, "Get the map out. Let's go find my brother."

CHAPTER 10

The past year had been the best year of Joshua Bailey's life. He had Lisa in his life, and they were getting closer and closer as the months went on. He, Lisa, Lance, and Becky would be seen together nearly every moment at school. They had become quite the foursome. On Thanksgiving, the Fisher family and the Bailey family celebrated the holiday at the Bailey farm. Nancy and Loanne made a feast for the families. Turkey, dressing, potatoes, and all the traditional makings of a perfect Thanksgiving. As with most gatherings on the holiday was customary, before partaking in the meal each person at the table was asked to share what they were thankful for. When it was Josh's turn, he paused for a moment then said, "I'm thankful for everyone at this table. Uncle Woody and Aunt Lo for everything they've done for me. I'm thankful that I have Lisa in my life and I'm thankful that Dan and Nancy have allowed me to date her." Everyone giggled at that. Especially Lisa's sister, Lori.

Josh continued, "Just before I arrived here, I had no family that I knew of. Now I am blessed to have two families. For that, I am extremely thankful."

* * *

Senior year went by quickly. Josh had recently turned eighteen. On that day, Woody and Lo asked Josh what his plans were now that he was a legal adult and could do whatever he wanted.

He said, "I want to stay here if you'll let me. I love it here and I enjoy working on the farm. I have no desire to move away. So, if you'll allow me to, I'd like to stay at least for a while."

Woody and Lo smiled at each other and then Woody said, "You can stay here as long as you want. We need you here and we want you here. We are both very proud of you and what you have overcome."

Lo said, "We both know that someday you'll need to be on your own. Hopefully, you and Lisa will get married someday and give us some great grandnieces and nephews. In the meantime, please do what you want. If that means staying here with us, then that's what you should do."

"I can't thank both of you enough for what you have done for me. You saved my life, and I'll never forget that. I couldn't have asked for a more loving, caring home than the one you both provided for me. I am eternally grateful to both of you." Josh said.

Lo and Woody smiled at each other. They had succeeded...admirably.

* * *

The telephone at the Bailey farm rang at 5:00 p.m. on a Thursday. Loanne answered and the female voice on the other end asked, "Is this the home of Josh Bailey?"

Lo said, "Yes, but he isn't here right now. Can I give him a message?"

The voice said, "My name is Emily Baker, and I have information that I need to share with him. Is he your nephew?"

Lo responded, "Yes, he is."

Emily asked, "When do you expect him home?"

"He should be here by 6:00. That's dinner time and he's never late for dinner."

Emily asked for directions to their home and if it would be alright for her and her friend to meet Josh there.

Lo obliged and gave Emily directions to the farm.

"Great. Thank you" Emily said, "We'll be there shortly."

Fifteen minutes later, Lo and Woody watched a green Camaro with Missouri license plates pull into the yard. Two young women who appeared to be in their twenties got out and walked up to the front porch. The one driving looked familiar but neither Lo nor Woody could be sure why. There was something about this woman that reminded them of someone, but they couldn't figure out who it was.

Lo greeted both ladies at the front door and invited them in.

Emily said, "Are you Loanne or Loanna Bailey?"

"Loanne. Most people call me Lo."

"I'm the one who called earlier," Emily said. "My name is Emily Baker, but my birth name is Emily Bailey."

* * *

A half-hour later, Lo, Woody, Emily, and Jessica were sitting at the kitchen table. The manilla envelope was resting on the table with Emily's birth certificate in front of her. The past half hour had been shocking for Woody and Lo. The information Emily gave them and showed them had their heads reeling.

Emily asked if Josh would be home soon. Woody said he should be there about any time. Just then they all heard Josh's Harley pull into the yard. Emily shot up from her seat and said, "Is that him?"

Lo and Woody nodded 'yes' and glanced warily at each other. Emily quickly went to the window to see her brother for the first time. She saw a young man on a Harley with a female riding with him. Their faces were obscured by the helmets they were both wearing. Emily was visibly shaking with nervousness and Jessica noticed. She said, "It'll be ok, Em. Take it easy. These are good people."

Lo said to Emily, "Please remember, he has no idea you exist. It will come as a shock to him just like it did for you when you found out about him. It's difficult to predict how he'll react."

"I understand," Emily said.

Josh and Lisa had been on the motorcycle all day. They were taking advantage of the time before the busy harvest that was coming soon. When they pulled into the farm they noticed a green Camaro with Missouri plates on it. Neither of them recognized the vehicle so they were curious to find out who it belonged to. They pulled the bike into the shop, got off, took their helmets off, and gave each other a little kiss. Coming through the kitchen door Josh said, "Who owns the badass Cam….." His voice stopped suddenly when he saw Emily standing near the table with Lo, Woody, and some other woman.

Lisa looked at Josh and said, "Babe, what is it? What's wrong?"

Emily slowly walked over to Josh and spoke. "Are you Joshua Bailey?"

Josh stood motionless and nodded 'yes.'

The woman said smiling, "This is going to be quite a shock for you and there's no easy way to say this, so I'll just say it. My name is Emily Baker, but my birth name is Emily Bailey. I'm your older sister."

Instant tears streamed down Josh's cheeks. He grabbed Emily and hugged her tightly. He said, "I knew it as soon as I saw your face. You look just like my mom."

"Our mom," Emily said while hugging Josh back.

Tears of happiness swept over the entire room. Even Uncle Woody had to wipe his eyes.

* * *

"We would love it if you both stayed for dinner." Lo said, "We're grilling steaks."

Emily and Jessica smiled at each other and Lo asked, "What is it?"

Emily said, "My adoptive parents own a steakhouse in St. Joseph."

Lo exclaimed, "Oh. Well then steaks aren't going to be much of a treat, are they?"

Emily laughed and said it was fine and they would be happy to stay for dinner.

The tears of happiness had finally subsided, and Josh and Emily decided to go out onto the porch to sit and talk. There was much to discuss.

Woody fired up the grill while Lo, Lisa, and Jessica prepared other food items in the kitchen and talked. They all felt it best to let Emily and Josh get to know each other by themselves. Sitting on the porch watching the tan wheat sway in the breeze across the road, Emily and Josh sat silently. Neither knew where to begin. Finally, Josh asked Emily, "How did you find me?"

Emily explained finding the manilla envelope and confronting her adoptive mother about its contents. Then she explained how she and Jessica traveled to Pleasanton looking for their mom. She told him about Sheriff Holts and the information he gave her about their mom's death.

Josh asked, "Holts is the Sheriff now?"

Emily replied, "Yeah, I guess. Why?"

"He was just a deputy when...well, you know," Josh said.

Emily nodded and went on to tell Josh about meeting Pastor Stevens.

"He was a good guy." Josh said, "He and his wife took me in right after mom died. How is he?"

"He's retired now," Emily said. "He told me to tell you that he wonders about you and that he hopes you're well. He's the one who suggested we look for you here."

There was a pause in the conversation. Emily said, "Do you have any pictures of our mom?"

Josh stood, dug his hand into his pocket, and retrieved the 5X7 photo that he had carried with him every day since the night their mom died. The photo was worn and creased but Emily was able to see her mom's face for the first time. Josh said, "This is the last picture taken of us together. It was taken the Christmas before she died."

Emily stared at the photo for a long moment and more tears began to well up in her eyes.

"Would you be willing to tell me about her?" She asked.

"Sure." Josh said, "What do you want to know?"

"Everything," Emily responded.

"Well," Josh began. "She was beautiful, like you. She was very kind. She never mistreated me or was abusive or anything like that. She went out with a lot of different guys. She drank but never to excess. I'm pretty sure she did drugs too, but I never saw her do anything first-hand. She never cooked big meals and didn't take very good care of the house we lived in. At the time, I didn't think anything of it. I just thought it was how everyone lived. Then when I got here and I got older, I realized that she was lost. She didn't know what she was doing. I loved her and I still do but it was not a good situation or home to be brought up in."

Emily said, "My mom, or I should say, my adoptive mom,

told me that she was doing drugs and partying a lot when they met her. She said that our mom had no money or anywhere to go because some guy she was with had dumped her off there when she was pregnant with me. She told me that our mom put me up for adoption when I was born. The couple who raised me did a great job. Sounds like I was lucky in some respects. Kind of like you. You have a good life here, don't you?"

"I've had a terrific life here. Uncle Woody and Aunt Lo are the best. They saved my life." Josh stated.

"It appears that everything has turned out for the best for both of us," Emily said.

"Well, other than our mother giving you up for adoption and being killed by an asshole she brought home, I'd say yeah, I guess," Josh said.

"It looks like I have a new Aunt and Uncle as well," Emily stated.

Josh said, "They are the best. No doubt about it."

A moment passed and Aunt Lo poked her head out the front door and announced that dinner was ready. Josh and Emily stood up and started toward the door. Josh said, "I'm so glad you found me, big sister."

Emily said, "Me too, little brother. Me too." and the two siblings entered the house.

* * *

They were all sitting at the table enjoying their steak dinners. There were many questions that needed answered but the conversation was lively and positive. When they all finished eating, they all went out onto the porch. Josh and Lisa were sitting on the porch swing while Woody, Lo, Emily, and Jessica were seated in chairs around the outdoor table. It was a warm and clear night. A slight south breeze was blowing and keeping temperatures from feeling too hot.

Josh asked Emily, "Did your adoptive mother tell you anything or know anything about your father?"

Emily said, "All she could remember was that the guy who left our mom, his name started with a 'B'. She was sure it was either Bill or Bruce or something like that."

The blood drained from Josh's face as he heard her mention the name, 'Bruce'. He rose quickly and said, "Excuse me for a minute" and ran down the stairs and back toward the shop.

Everyone had a quizzical look on their faces. Lisa stood up and ran after Josh. When she caught up with him, she found him in the shop pacing back and forth mumbling something. She asked, "Josh, what's wrong? What happened?"

Josh still pacing said, "Bruce. She said the name 'Bruce'."

"Okay," Lisa said. "What about him?"

Woody came into the shop and asked, "What's going on?"

Josh said, "Emily said her dad's name was Bruce."

Woody said, "Okay. And?"

Josh said, "Don't you see? Bruce was the name of the guy who killed my mom. The same guy I shot in the head."

Woody said, "Oh, shit."

"I'm certain that I killed our dad," Josh exclaimed.

"You mean this Bruce guy was yours AND Emily's dad?" Lisa asked.

"Yes," Josh said frantically. "It's all coming back to me now.

I've read about suppressed memories and things that could trigger them. I remember everything now. The fight, what they said to each other, all of it."

He looked at Uncle Woody and said, "The night my mom died, the man who killed her said something to me that I couldn't understand at the time. He said, "I'm your fa.… ". That's when I shot him."

"Oh my god," Lisa said.

Woody said, "Are you absolutely sure?"

"Yes. I'm positive. My mom said something too that I couldn't understand at the time either but now it's like I can hear her say it. She said, 'He's your father'." Josh said quietly. "And another thing, during their fight my mom said, "I told you that if you ever hit me again you were out." He was breathing hard. The realization and details of what happened that night were flooding over him.

"So, he had hit her before?" Woody asked.

Josh snapped back, "Yes, but here's the thing. I had never met him before that night. As far as I knew, neither had my mom. He must be Emily's dad and mine too."

Josh resumed pacing, hitting his head with his hand and mumbling those phrases repeatedly. Lisa ran to him and tried to calm him down. "It's okay, Sweetie. It's going to be alright."

Josh said, "I killed my own father and Emily's father too. This will never be okay."

Woody rushed to him, grabbed his shoulders, and held him tight. "Take it easy, there's no way you could have known. Listen to me. You didn't do anything wrong."

Woody looked at Lisa with a concerned look on his face. She came to them and took over, holding Josh for Woody.

After a few seconds, Josh walked over to an old rocking chair that was sitting in the corner of the shop. He sat with his head in his hands rocking back and forth rapidly. He said, "What do I do? Do I tell Emily that I killed our father?"

Woody said, "We'll figure it out." He looked at Lisa and said, "I'll be right back. Lisa, stay with him, please." Then he walked out of the shop and back toward the front porch.

Lisa said, "I will. I'm not going anywhere." She looked at Josh and began to cry. She was very worried about him. Not sure what to say, all she could do was wait until he asked for her. She felt utterly helpless.

* * *

After a few minutes, Josh was finally beginning to settle down. His rocking had decreased, and he was able to look Lisa in the eye. He said, "I'm reliving the nightmare."

Lisa went to him and knelt in front of him. She said, "I know, Sweetheart. I'm here for you if you need anything."

"Would you just stay here with me?" He asked her.

"Of course I will. Whatever you need."

Josh reached out to her and hugged her as tightly as he could. Lisa returned the hug and told him. "I love you, Joshua Bailey."

He said, "I love you, Lisa Fisher."

Aunt Lo entered the shop, and she found them both hugging in the corner. She walked over to them and said, "Josh, Honey. Are you alright?"

"I don't know what to do." He replied.

Lo said, "Woody told us what you said. It's okay. Emily is alright. She understands. She doesn't blame you."

"Are you sure? It's a terrible thing that I did. I took our father away from both of us." Josh said.

Lo said, "I'm positive. You need to go to your sister. You have nothing to apologize for. She's waiting for you on the porch."

Josh slowly got up from the rocking chair and took Lisa's hand into his. The three of them walked back toward the porch. Emily came running down the stairs and put her arms around Josh. She said, "Uncle Woody told me everything. It's okay. We're going to be alright."

"I'm so sorry," Josh said, "I took our father away from both of us."

"You did exactly what you had to do. No one is blaming you for any of it. Not me. Not anyone. There is nothing to forgive except for yourself. You must forgive yourself, little brother." Emily said.

Josh held his sister in his arms for a long moment. "Thank you, Sis. I'll try."

An hour later, Loanne told Emily and Jessica that they were more than welcome to stay with them for as long as they needed. They had plenty of space. Em and Jessica thanked her and said they would like that. They'll need to head back to St. Joseph the next day.

Josh walked Lisa to her car which was parked outside the shop. He said, "It's been a hell of a day, hasn't it?"

Lisa smiled and said, "Yeah, it has. Are you going to be alright?"

Josh said, "Yeah. Thank you for being here and helping me through this. You're my hero."

Lisa smiled again and said, "Anything for my hero."

They kissed each other goodbye then Lisa got in her car and drove to town.

Josh went back up to the porch which was now empty and sat on the porch swing. After a few moments, Uncle Woody came out of the house and sat down next to Josh. Josh said, "Thank you for what you did tonight, Uncle Woody. I owe you."

Woody said, "You don't owe me a thing, Buddy. I'm just glad you're ok."

"What a day," Josh proclaimed.

Woody said, "That's an understatement."

The two of them sat in silence watching the sun go down.

The basement at the Bailey home had been set up with two large beds. Lo made sure the girls would have everything they needed. It was a spacious room with a television and a few decorations on the walls. She announced, "If you need anything, please let me know. It's good to have guests. Especially when they're family. That includes you too, Jessica."

The girls smiled and thanked Lo for everything. When Lo exited back up the stairs, Jessica asked Emily, "How are you holding up?"

Emily answered, "Better than I thought I would be. Thank you for coming with me."

Jessica said, "This has been one of the craziest few days of my life. It's like being in the middle of a soap opera. I wouldn't have missed it for the world."

Emily said. "I'm glad we came here. These people are my true blood family, and they seem very nice."

"What about Josh?" Jessica asked,

"I think he's a wonderful little brother," Emily replied. "He seems to be very well-adjusted, smart and considerate. I hate to imagine that night when our mom died. What it must have been like for him. He was only twelve years old for Christ's sake."

"Yeah", Jessica agreed. "Think about this too. His mom dies, he kills the man who took her life, and he has no family at the time. No one to lean on or take care of him. Then he meets his aunt and Uncle whom he didn't even know about and moves to a strange town. Then years later he realizes that the man he shot was your guys' father. I can't imagine what that would feel like. Now out of the blue, he has a sister that he didn't know existed. Both of you have been through one hell of a day."

The following morning, Lo and Woody were up before dawn. Woody made a pot of coffee while Loanne busied herself preparing to feed a houseful of people breakfast. She was in her element. She loved to cook for people and now she had two extra mouths to feed. She was enjoying every minute of it.

Woody was seated at the kitchen table nursing his first cup of coffee and Lo noticed he was deep in thought. She said, "What's on your mind?"

"You realize we now have a new grand-niece?" He spoke.

"I know," Lo responded. "It sure does explain a lot, doesn't it."

Woody said, "I can't believe my brother kicked Angel out of the house. That's eating at me."

"You know how he was." She spoke. "Drinking all the time and abusing her when she was a kid."

"I know but why couldn't he tell us the truth about where Angel was," Woody said agitated. "We would've helped her."

Lo said, "Maybe that's why. Maybe he didn't want anyone to help her, maybe he was too embarrassed about the whole situation. Unfortunately, we'll never know."

"I have to say, I'm happy Emily found us, and I know she and Josh are happy to have found each other too," Woody exclaimed. "I'm worried about him, though. His revelation last night and having that flashback and all. That was tough to watch."

Lo said, "Yeah but remember, we both did a great job with him. He's a levelheaded kid and he's smart. He'll be just fine. I know he will."

A moment later, Emily and Jessica appeared in the kitchen. Everyone said "good morning" to each other. Lo asked if they were hungry. Em and Jessica both nodded and said, "Absolutely."

Woody said, "Lo is the best cook in the entire county and if anyone says otherwise, they'll have to reckon with me."

The girls smiled and Emily said, "Somehow I don't doubt that."

Lo told them there's coffee ready if they would like some and breakfast will be finished cooking soon.

The girls took seats at the table with their cups and Emily asked, "Is Josh up yet?"

Woody said, "No, not yet. He had an exciting day yesterday. We all did."

Emily asked, "May I ask? What is he like? What kind of person is he?"

Lo said, "He's mostly quiet. He reads a lot. He's a hard worker and he got good grades in school." She glanced at Woody, and he winked at her because he was sure what she would say next. She said, "He's very protective."

"Of what?" Emily asked.

"Of everyone that he cares about and some he doesn't even know," Woody said. "Let me tell you a story…". He told them about what Josh had done back in the seventh grade with Sam Blackwell and Witch Hazel.

"So, I take it he doesn't like bullies," Emily exclaimed.

Lo said, "He hates them. We're sure it goes back to the night your mom died and probably even before that."

Lo then told the story of Josh's confrontation with Lisa's ex-boyfriend and how they got together. Emily and Jessica listened intently to the stories. "He's an amazing young man and we are very proud of him. He's never been a problem for us, and we are blessed to have him." Lo explained.

Woody chimed in, "Now we are blessed to have a newly discovered niece too."

Emily and Jessica smiled at that. Emily said, "I'm so glad I found all of you. This has turned out to be better than I could have expected. Thank you both so much for being so kind to us."

* * *

An hour later, Josh walked slowly and quietly down the stairs and toward the kitchen where he found the four of them looking through an old photo album. Loanne was pointing at pictures and describing who the people were. "And this is your mom on her sixteenth birthday." She looked at Woody and she spoke, "That was the last time we saw her."

Jessica said, "She was very pretty."

Josh spoke up and startled everyone when he said. "Yes, she was."

They hadn't seen or heard him coming down the stairs so when he spoke it jarred them a bit.

"Good morning," Josh said. He looked at Emily and asked, "How'd you sleep, Sis?"

"Honestly," Emily replied. "Not that well. Too much information has been going through my mind the past few days. It's a lot to take in."

Josh said, "Yeah, same here."

Josh grabbed a plate and began loading up with that amazing bacon, eggs, and hash browns. He said, "What do think of our Aunt Lo's cooking?"

Jessica said, "It's amazing. We could use her at the steakhouse. And Woody too."

"Well, you can't have her." Josh quipped with a smile on his face. "She's staying right where she is if I have anything to say about it. They both are. They can't be traipsing off to St. Joseph." He smiled when he said it. "I need them here."

* * *

"I guess we better be getting back," Emily announced an hour later. "I need to get the steakhouse back open since we shut it down after my adoptive father died."

Lo said, "Thank you so much for seeking out Josh. He may not say it, but he's very happy to have a sister now. And we're happy to have a new niece also."

Woody said, "What Lo said. If you ever need anything, don't hesitate to call. We'll be there for you."

Josh walked down the stairs of the front porch with Emily and Jessica. When they got to the Camaro, he said, "I'm so glad you searched for me and found me. If you ever need anything, and I mean ANYTHING, you let me know and I'll be there. That goes for you too, Jessica."

"I will", Emily said. "Take care of yourself and let me hear from you."

"I want to talk to you at least once a week," Josh responded.

"Absolutely," Emily exclaimed. "You got it, little bro."

They hugged and the girls climbed into the car, Josh leaned his head into the driver's side window and said, "Take good care of my sister, Jessica. She's very important to me."

"I certainly will, Josh. Count on it." Jessica replied.

"Call me when you get home, please. I'm a worrier." He spoke.

"We will, I promise," Emily said.

"Lisa and I will be up to visit when harvest is done." He announced.

"Excellent, I can't wait." Emily said, "Love you, little brother."

"Love you too, big Sis."

Emily started the Camaro and drove out of the yard and back toward St. Joseph. Josh watched silently as they drove away waving his hand high in the air.

CHAPTER 11

Later that afternoon, Woody and Josh were piddling around in the shop getting the combine ready for harvest. Make sure it had an oil change and was greased up properly. The two of them had done this routine so many times over the past few years that Woody didn't have to tell Josh what to do next. They worked well as a team. Woody knew that Josh was more than capable of getting any chores done without his supervision.

"So, what's your plan for tonight? Are you and Lisa going out? Is she staying the night?", Woody asked.

It had become a common thing for Lisa to stay over on Friday or Saturday nights. Both Dan and Nancy as well as Lo and Woody had no problem with the two of them sleeping in the same bed. They all knew what Josh and Lisa would most likely be engaged in and were fine with it. After all, they were both eighteen and smart enough to use caution. Plus, they would rather they do that in their home rather than in the back of the pick-up or in some field somewhere.

Josh said, "Yeah. We're meeting up with Lance and Becky at Pizza Hut then maybe go to the bowling alley. Then Lisa will stay here tonight." He continued, "I talked to Lance earlier, and he said they have something important they want to talk to us about. He's being very secretive. Makes me kind of worried."

Woody said, "Maybe they're getting married or something."

Josh said, "I don't know. Maybe."

The Pizza Hut in Anthony was just like anywhere else. The aroma of freshly baked breadsticks and pizza dough wafted over the entire restaurant. All the tables had red and white vinyl, and checkered tablecloths on them. Josh, Lisa, Becky, and Lance were seated in a booth and had just ordered a large pan-crust meat lover's pizza. They did that because they knew Josh hated vegetables. Josh would always insist that they get what they wanted and not change their eating habits just because he was picky.

Lance spoke up, "So what's new?"

Lisa and Josh smiled at each other and Josh said, "Go ahead and tell them. I know you want to."

Lisa said, "Yes, I do." She looked at Lance and Becky and said, "We had quite a surprise yesterday." She told them about Emily and her friend Jessica and how they found Josh. She said, "Josh has a sister he didn't know about. It was quite a shock."

Becky and Lance looked at Josh. Becky said, "Holy crap. What's she like?"

Josh said, "She looks just like my mom, and she sounds like her too."

Lance said, "That's the craziest story I've ever heard."

Lisa and Josh had decided earlier not to tell them about Josh's revelation and flashback. They didn't need to hear that part.

Lisa said, "It was so emotional. When Josh first looked at her, his jaw dropped, and he knew right away that she had to be his sister even before she told him. It was a moment I'll never forget."

Becky said, "That is an amazing story. Where does she live?"

Josh said, "She owns a steakhouse in St. Joseph."

"Wow", Lance exclaimed. "That is so cool that she found you."

Josh replied, "Yeah, it is" He asked, "So what is it you wanted to tell us?"

Lance looked at Becky and she smiled back at him and nodded her head.

"We're leaving town. Moving to Wichita." Lance announced.

"What? When?", Josh asked.

"Tomorrow," Lance replied.

"Tomorrow?" Josh said loudly. "Why so soon?"

Becky said, "We each found jobs there. Lance found a job

working at a music store selling guitars. I'm going to work at a clothing store at Towne West."

Josh said, "I don't understand the urgency."

Lance said, "We've been planning this and saving up for months. We have an apartment all setup."

Lisa had sat quietly during the exchange. She could feel Josh's gaze. He said, "You knew about this didn't you?"

"I did," Lisa answered sheepishly.

"Why didn't you tell me?" Josh said.

Lance spoke up, "Don't blame her. We made her promise not to tell you. We asked her to wait until we could talk to you in person."

"I'm sorry, Sweetie," Lisa said.

Josh sat in stunned silence shaking his head back and forth. Too much has happened over the past two days. Both were good things, but it still was a lot to absorb.

Lance said, "Are you okay, Buddy?"

Josh said, "I'm fine. I'm just surprised. I thought you guys were getting married or something."

Lisa asked, "Are you mad at me for not telling you?"

"Of course not," Josh replied. "It would take a lot more than that for me to get mad at you. A lot more."

Lance said, "We need to get away from here. I'm never going to get a band started here. Becky and I are just following our hearts and our dreams. We need this and we'd really appreciate your support and understanding".

Josh said, "You know I would support anything you two want to do. I'm happy for you both. I understand what you're doing and why you're doing it. I'm just going to miss you guys. I know Lisa will too."

Becky said, "We won't be far away. It's not like we're going to New York or anything."

"Yeah." Josh said, "We can see you on weekends from time to time."

Their pizza arrived and they began eating. The four of them told stories and reminisced about different tales from when they were kids. They laughed and talked until the pizza was gone.

The Anthony bowling alley was relatively small compared to the ones in the city. It had only 20 lanes, a few video games, and a small, enclosed bar at the far end of it. It reeked of stale cigarette smoke and the white ceiling tiles were stained brown from the smoke that wafted up to them. On Friday and Saturday nights, it was busy. Most of the lanes were taken up with families and couples out for a night of fun and relaxation. Between the movie theater and the bowling alley, the residents of the small town had only those two places they could go to have a little fun.

On this night, Josh, Lisa, Becky, and Lance had been able to acquire lane three and were having fun rolling the balls down the lane. The sound of the pins being hit echoed throughout the lanes. They were bowling next to another foursome that they knew so it was a good time. Josh and Lisa were determined to show Becky and Lance a fun time on their last night in town. Then at one point, Lisa and Becky excused themselves and said they were going to use the restroom.

Lance said to Josh, "Why is it that the girls always go to the bathroom together?"

Josh laughed and said, "I honestly do not know. It's a mystery that goes back a thousand years. I'll bet Cleopatra used the facilities with other women all the time."

Lance laughed and said, "I sure am going to miss your sense of humor and observations."

In small communities throughout the country, there would be at least one person who was known as the 'town drunk'. In Anthony, that person was Al Fredericks. Known all over town as 'Drunk Al'. He was a large, burly man. He weighed at least 250 pounds and stood 6'5". He always wore the same oil-soaked jeans and a snap button shirt that was constantly open down to his big beer belly and he wore a torn ball cap that appeared to have been run over by a lawnmower. He had a shaggy, dark beard that always seemed to have food crumbs lodged in it. He was grotesque, abrasive, mean, and very loud. Josh knew of him but fortunately never had to engage with him in any way. Everyone in town feared him and avoided him as much as possible.

Drunk Al staggered his way out of the bar at the far end of the bowling alley. He immediately began shouting insults at the bowlers on the opposite end from where Josh and Lance were waiting for the girls to return.

Lance noticed him first and said, "Oh shit. It's drunk Al."

Josh turned to see Al weaving back and forth and calling the other bowlers vile names and harassing them saying things like "You suck at bowling" and "You couldn't bowl your way out of a wet paper bag." He even went so far as to call a small boy who was out with his family a "little pussy".

"Goddammit," Josh said. "I hate that guy."

Just then Lisa and Becky exited the restroom and Al noticed them. He staggered over to them and said to Becky. "Hey, little darlin'. Why don't you and I go out behind the building so we can fuck."

Becky said, "No fucking way."

Al grabbed her by her arm and said, "You're coming with me."

Becky kicked him as hard as she could in his shin and Al reared back and backhanded Becky across her face. Lisa caught Becky and they both walked quickly away while Josh and Lance ran over to confront drunk Al. The other bowlers were shocked at what they saw and some of them eased their way closer to the action. The desk clerk at the other end of the building was on the phone. Hopefully calling the police.

Lance and Josh came to within 5 five feet of Al. Lance said, "What the fuck is wrong with you?" Then he made the mistake of turning his head to look at Becky.

Al stepped closer to Lance swung hard with his huge, right hand, and connected with Lance's jaw. Lance went down hard onto the floor. Josh placed himself in between Al and Lance. He was glaring at Al and said, "You just made a huge mistake, Al."

"Fuck you, little boy," and took a swing at Josh. Josh ducked and Al's fist went over Josh's head. Josh immediately raised back up and with three very fast jabs punched the bigger man in his nose, POP POP POP. Then another fast jab to Al's throat. Blood spewed from drunk Al's nose, and he was choking. Next, Josh moved to his left, raised his knee up near his own chest, and rammed the sole of his boot into the side of Al's knee knocking it out of its socket. Al hit the floor with a large thud grimacing and groaning in pain. The onlookers were in complete shock at what they were seeing. Josh looked down at drunk Al and said, "Are you done?"

Al was choking and he mumbled something. Josh asked again, "I said, are you done?" in a loud voice. Al had one hand over his now broken nose with blood running into his hand and his other hand gripping his now shattered knee. Al nodded his head as if to say 'yes'. Josh quickly went to Becky and Lance. He said, "Are you guys, okay?"

Lance said, "Yeah. We're alright."

Josh looked at Lisa and saw her shrug and almost smile. Josh shook his head and said, "Fucking asshole."

Drunk Al lay on the floor and tried to get up, but his dislocated knee prevented him from being successful. Still in shock, the small group that had gathered stood in silence staring at the large heap lying on the floor. The little boy who Al had moments before called a little pussy broke the silence. He pointed at Al's crotch and said, "Look, Dad. That man peed his pants."

Laughter erupted from the onlookers as well as Lisa, Becky, and Lance. The only one not laughing was Josh.

* * *

Police officer, Scott Wilkenson arrived a few moments later. Officer Wilkenson was very well-liked in town. He was known to be very fair and easy to talk to. Everyone in town had much respect for him. He never abused his authority and had a great sense of humor. He was tall and handsome.

He looked sharp in his uniform and carried himself confidently yet humbly at the same time. When he arrived at the bowling alley, he stopped at the front desk and the desk clerk pointed down to the other end of the building. Officer Wilkenson made his way to where the crowd was beginning to break up. He glanced over and saw Lance, Becky, Lisa, and Josh all sitting at a table waiting and watching. He walked over to where Al was lying on the floor. Al, now able to speak said, "Wilkenson, get me up from here."

Officer Wilkenson said, "Not yet. You look comfortable down there. It's a good place for you. Besides, you look like you need the rest." Then he asked loudly enough for everyone to hear. "Who wants to tell me what happened?"

Lisa said, "I will".

Officer Wilkenson walked over to where the four friends were seated. Lisa stood and explained everything that had happened. Wilkenson looked around and asked if anyone disagreed with what Lisa had told him. One person said that it happened just like Lisa said.

He asked Josh, "Is that what happened?"

Josh replied, "That's exactly what happened. Are you going to arrest me?"

Wilkenson said, "No. You guys are free to go if you want to."

They all looked at each other, stood up, and started toward the door.

Scott Wilkenson walked back over to where Al was still lying. He said, "Looks like you've had a rough night, Al. Here's what's going to happen. You get to go for a ride in an ambulance to the hospital. Then after they get you cleaned up and fixed up, you're going to jail. How does that sound?"

"Fuck you, Wilkenson." was Al's reply.

Officer Wilkenson laughed and said, "You finally got what was coming to you after all these years. Karma's a bitch, isn't it?"

Al said, "Whatever."

Wilkenson laughed again and said, "You know the next time you go out drinking, and that will be a long time from now, maybe you should wear a diaper."

* * *

Josh, Lisa, Becky, and Lance were standing outside the bowling alley. Josh said, "I think I've had all the fun I can stand for one night."

The others chuckled and agreed. Josh asked Becky and Lance if they were going to be okay. They both nodded.

Becky said, "That was the most amazing thing I've ever seen, Josh. Thank you for what you did."

Lance said, "Yeah. Thanks, buddy. I owe you."

"You don't have to thank me. Neither one of you." Josh said. "You made a mistake in there, Lance. You took your eyes from drunk Al. That's what got you. I'm not saying it's your fault at all. Just next time remember, never take your eyes off your opponent until he's down or unconscious."

"Lesson learned, my friend," Lance replied.

Lisa said, "I'm sorry your last night in town ended like this."

Becky said. "Don't be. We had a great time and now we have a story to tell that we'll never forget."

Josh said, "Please take care of each other and yourselves. You're both very important to us. Lisa and I wish you the best of luck and all the happiness you can find."

They all hugged each other and said their goodbyes.

* * *

Later that night after making love, Lisa and Josh were catching their breath. Josh had his arm around her shoulder and Lisa's head was resting comfortably on Josh's chest. After a few moments, she asked, "Why do you hate alcohol so much?"

Josh said, "I don't hate alcohol. I think everyone has the right to drink as much as they want so long as the effects don't cause anyone else harm. Most people who drink are happy, fun-loving folks. But there are those very few that allow the booze to make them mean or hateful or worse yet, violent. It's not the alcohol I don't like. It's the people who allow it to change them into monsters that they wouldn't be if they were sober."

Lisa thought for a moment and said, "Do your feelings on it go back to your mom?'

Without hesitation, Josh said, "Yes."

Lisa said, "You know when that little boy announced that Drunk Al had peed his pants?"

"Yeah"

"Why weren't you laughing? Everyone else was."

Josh said, "Because I'm the one who made it happen. To me, there was nothing funny about it."

CHAPTER 12

The wheat harvest that year went on without a hitch. Woody and Lo were very pleased with the yield they received from it. They made very good money and nothing overly pricy happened. Woody said it was the most productive harvest they had ever had. Over the next month, the fields would be prepared for planting next year's crop, and by the time September arrived, things to do at the farm decreased which enabled Josh to spend more time with Lisa. They made occasional trips to Wichita to visit Becky and Lance. Lance had found some guys to jam with and they were working up set lists to be performed at local bars in and around Wichita. Meanwhile, Becky was enjoying her job at the clothing store. Her outgoing personality shined through, and she became quite successful as a salesperson. Life was good for both, and Josh and Lisa were happy for them. Josh told Lance that he needed to let them know when and where their first gig would be. He and Lisa would be there.

On Thanksgiving that year the Fisher's and Bailey's once again celebrated at the Bailey farm. Christmas was exciting for Josh. He had two families to celebrate with. When he was a child, he felt fortunate to get a small present from his mom. He didn't complain, he knew money was hard to come by for her. Both the Fisher's and the Bailey's would get him wonderful gifts.

He also had fun shopping for everyone. He and Lisa would go to Wichita to find things that were unavailable in town plus it gave them an opportunity to see Becky and Lance in their working environments. They enjoyed showing up at their respective stores and surprising them.

When Josh had turned fourteen, Woody and Lo would travel to Kansas City for New Year's Eve. They would make the long drive up, stay in a nice hotel, and dance the night away before returning on January 2nd or 3rd. This year would be no different except that Woody and Lo left on December 29th instead of the 31st. They told Josh that they wanted to spend a little more time in Kansas City before New Year's Eve this year. When December 31st arrived, Josh and Lisa decided to celebrate the New Year at the farm watching rented movies and having a pleasant meal alone. They both enjoyed the peacefulness in the country. No traffic or bright lights outside.

It was indeed cold but fortunately, there was no snow on the ground on this New Year.

Lovemaking that night was different for both. Not worse

than before but...different, better. Something in their minds and feelings made their sex this time more passionate than ever before. The touching, caressing, and hand holding was more intense than it had ever been. They both climaxed simultaneously with Lisa on top of Josh. Writing, moaning, sweating. They looked deeply into each other's eyes as their lovemaking reached its glorious peak.

Exhausted, they lay in bed still panting from the intense physical activity they had placed their bodies through. Josh glanced at his alarm clock and said, "Damn. It's 12:05. We missed ringing in the new year."

Lisa chuckled and said, "I disagree. I think we brought it in extremely well if you ask me."

"You are absolutely right, my lady," Josh said. "I stand corrected." Then they kissed with more passion and feeling than they ever had.

Josh said after the kiss finally broke off, "Happy New Year, Lisa. I love you very much."

Lisa replied, "I love you more, my hero."

After a moment, Lisa said, "I hope this is an indication that 1989 will be a good year. It certainly has started off that way."

"It sure has," Josh replied. "It most assuredly has."

They both fell into a deep sleep. Each of them with a smile on their face.

* * *

On Valentine's Day, Josh presented Lisa with a necklace. It had a simple gold chain and the figure of an Angel as a pendant. When he gave it to her, he said, "This belonged to my mom. I want you to have it. I've been saving it since the night she passed away."

Lisa opened the small box and when she saw the angel attached to it, she gasped. She said, "I can't accept this, Babe. It belongs with you."

Josh knew she would respond this way, and he said, "You belong with me and the necklace belongs with you. I insist you take it. Mom would have wanted it to be worn by someone that I love."

A tear came down Lisa's cheek as Josh placed the necklace around her subtle neck. He kissed her neck and had her turn around so he could see how it looked on her. "Perfect." He spoke.

Lisa said, "This is the most wonderful gift I've ever received. Thank you, Sweetie."

"You're welcome, Lisa."

A week later, Uncle Woody, Aunt Loanne, and Josh were seated at the kitchen table eating dinner. Outside the sky was gray and a light snow was beginning to fall. It was very serene.

When they had all finished eating, Lo said, "Josh, we have something to tell you."

Josh looked at both and the looks on their faces gave him an uneasy feeling.

He said, "Okay. What's up?

Lo glanced at Woody who was sitting still, his head was bent down with his eyes looking down at the table.

Lo hesitated and Josh knew something bad was about to happen.

"What's going on? You're scaring me." He said.

Lo looked at Josh and said, "You remember when Woody and I went to Kansas City for New Year and how we left a couple of days sooner than we usually do?"

Josh nodded 'yeah'.

"Well," Lo said. "We went to see a doctor in Wichita on the way. They needed to run some tests on Woody. Josh, honey, your Uncle Woody has prostate cancer."

Josh quickly looked at his uncle. Woody's head was still bowed. He said, "Oh my god. So, what are they going to do? How do we fix it?"

Woody raised his head slowly and said, "There's not much they can do. The Doc says it's too far advanced. We didn't get tested soon enough. He said they could try chemo and radiation, but it would only prolong the inevitable. It wouldn't cure it."

Josh said, "Bullshit. There must be something they can do. Anything."

Lo looked at Josh with tears streaming down her beautiful face. All she could do was shake her 'no'.

Josh shot up out of his chair and shouted, "FUCK" and then ran down the stairs and out to the shop.

* * *

A few moments later, Uncle Woody found Josh in the rocking chair in the shop. He was rocking back and forth rapidly while looking down at the shop floor. Woody walked over to him and said, "I'm sorry, son, but you needed to know."

Josh said, "Well it's not true. This is not happening."

Woody said, "I know how you feel, buddy. I know you're angry and hurting inside."

"You have to fight this," Josh said loudly. "You cannot quit. You must do everything you can to stay alive. I'll do whatever it takes to help. I don't care what it is."

Woody, who rarely sheds a tear could not prevent it this time. He felt worse for Josh than he did for himself at that moment. He said, "I know how hard this is for you. It's hard for me and your aunt Lo too. We need you, Josh. Now more than ever."

Josh jumped up out of the rocking chair and wrapped his arms around his uncle holding him tightly. "I'm so sorry, Uncle Woody. I hate this so much."

Woody returned the hug, squeezing Josh hard. "I know you do. So do we."

"Whatever you and Aunt Lo need me to do, I'll do it. It doesn't matter what it is, I'll do it." Josh said emphatically.

Lo made her way silently into the shop and saw her two men hugging near the rocking chair. She could see and feel their pain. She turned and slowly made her way back into the house. When she got to the kitchen, she went about cleaning up from dinner like she always did. Rinsing off the dishes and silverware and placing the items into the dishwasher. As she began wiping the table, her emotions got the best of her. She plopped down in her chair and sobbed uncontrollably with her beautiful face in her soft hands.

* * *

The three of them sat quietly back at the kitchen table. It had been an hour since Lo's announcement. They all were in a state of shock and disbelief.

Finally, Josh asked, "Who else knows?"

Lo said, "Just the three of us and the doctor."

"Someone needs to tell Dan, Nancy, and Lisa, and I need to call Emily," Josh said.

Loanne said, "Would you be okay with calling them?"

Josh said, "I'll do better than that. I'll tell them in person. It would be better that way, don't you think?"

Woody nodded his head in agreement. Lo said, "That's a good idea."

"The snow has let up," Josh said as he rose. "I'll call Lisa and let her know I'm on my way then I'll head to town. First, I need to call Emily."

* * *

After talking to Emily and sharing the news with her, Josh bundled up in his heavy winter coat and went downstairs. Lo and Woody were still at the kitchen table sitting silently. Josh passed by them and said, "I'll be back in a little while. Do you guys need anything while I'm in town?"

Lo and Woody both shook their heads 'no'. Lo said, "Be careful."

"I will," Josh said and he walked down the stairs and into the shop.

Once he left, Woody said to Lo, "We need to talk about things for when I'm gone."

Lo said, "I know. Can we do that tomorrow? I think Josh should be here for that discussion, don't you?"

Woody said, "I suppose he should be. For some of it."

* * *

Josh arrived at the Fisher home at 8:00. It was dark and cold. The streets of Anthony were quiet. Lisa answered the door and Josh went inside, removed his coat, and gave her a kiss. He said, "I need to talk to you. All of you if I could."

"Something's wrong. I can tell." Lisa said.

Josh said, "Would you bring everyone into your dad's den, please?"

"Of course." She replied.

Josh walked into Dan's den and waited while Lisa gathered the rest of her family and brought them into the room. Dan sat at his desk and Lori and Nancy sat in the same chairs that Josh and Nancy had sat in just before his first date with Lisa. Josh and Lisa remained standing.

Dan said, "What's wrong, Josh?"

Josh said, "I don't know an easy way to tell you all this, so I guess the best way is to just say it." Each of the family members had looks of concern on their faces. Josh continued, "Uncle Woody has been diagnosed with prostate cancer."

"Oh, dear god", Nancy said.

"Damn." Said Dan. "When did he find out?"

Josh said, "Apparently he and Aunt Lo got the test results back today."

Lisa said, crying, "I'm so sorry, Babe"

There was a moment of silence. The family was trying to take it all in. Lori had tears forming in her eyes as did the rest of the family.

Josh said, "I volunteered to come and tell you in person. I thought it would be better than calling."

Dan said, "We appreciate that, Josh. What's the prognosis?"

Josh explained what Woody had told him earlier. Then he said, "It doesn't look good."

Lisa hugged her hero and said, "Thank you for coming and telling us."

Nancy said, "Yes, thank you for doing this."

Dan asked, "How is Lo holding up?"

Josh told them that she appeared to be okay, but he was sure that she was having a rough time with it.

Dan said, "That's to be expected."

Josh said, "I better get back home in case they need something. I'm sorry for having to bring you bad news."

Nancy said, "Don't apologize for that. We all appreciate you coming here and telling us. If you guys need anything, please let us know."

Josh said, "Thanks" then grabbed his coat, put it on, and started toward the front door with Lisa holding his hand.

He looked at her and said, "This sucks, so bad."

"I know, Babe. I'm here for you and Woody and Lo. Whatever you need."

"Thank you, Sweetheart. I'll call you tomorrow. I love you." He said.

"I love you too," Lisa responded.

Josh walked out into the cold to the pickup, started the

engine, and drove away. As he drove back to the farm, he remembered many of the things Woody had taught him but the memory that stood out mostly in Josh's mind was...one shot.

* * *

Over the next few months, there were many visits to the doctor's office. Sometimes Josh would go with them but usually Woody would insist that Josh stay home and do the normal farm chores. As he promised, Josh would do anything that Woody and Lo needed him to do. For Woody, that meant taking care of the farm. Doing the work was good for Josh. It helped keep his mind off Woody's cancer and the treatments he was going through. He still held out hope for Woody to get better. He was convinced that his uncle would be okay.

Lisa would come to the house nearly every day after working at her father's store. Sometimes she would spend the night so she could be with Josh as much as possible and assist Lo with whatever she needed. Lisa tried very hard to make things on the Bailey's as easy and comfortable as possible. Nancy and Dan would visit at least once a week to check on their friends. Nancy would bring meals so Lo wouldn't have to cook much, and it allowed Lo to concentrate her time on helping Woody.

It was a difficult and emotionally exhausting time for all of them.

* * *

In late May, five weeks after Josh's nineteenth birthday, Woody was admitted to the hospital. All the treatments that were being utilized had some effect but not enough. Woody was frail, weak, and had trouble just getting around. His red hair was gone from the massive amounts of chemicals he was given. The cancer had spread to his bones. The doctor informed Lo and Josh that the cancer was in stage four and there was nothing more they could do to stop the spread. They were left with only one option, to give Woody as much pain medicine as he could tolerate to make him as comfortable as possible. The pain meds made him sleep most of the time.

One afternoon not long after Woody was admitted to the hospital, Josh was in his uncle's room with him. Sitting in a chair and watching his uncle sleep. Josh still had trouble dealing with the potential loss of his uncle, but he never gave up hope.

Woody's eyes opened slowly, and he glanced at Josh. Woody said, "Where's Lo?"

Josh told him that Lo had gone to the house but would be right back. "How are you feeling, Uncle Woody?" Josh asked.

Woody smiled and said, "Tired". He continued, his voice was raspy and soft. "It's probably good that Lo isn't here. I need to talk to you while I'm awake."

Josh said, "I'm right here. What can I do for you?"

"I need you to listen to me," Woody said nearly in a whisper. "I need you to promise me something."

"Anything."

Woody said, "I need you to take care of your Aunt Lo for me. Will you do that?"

Josh answered, "Of course, I will. But you don't need me to promise that. You'll be out of here soon."

Woody shook his head and said, "This is my time, Josh. Remember what I told you about having one shot? This is what I meant. Right here. Right now." He paused then said, "Marry Lisa, Josh. Raise a family. Take care of the people you love. You've grown into an outstanding man and I'm so proud of you. I tried to raise you like I would my own son."

Josh had tears running down his face and he said. "You did great Uncle Woody. You saved my life. You taught me everything I need to know to be as much like you as possible."

Woody raised his hand and Josh grabbed it. He bent down closer to Woody.

Woody whispered in Josh's ear, "Be better than me."

Two days later Josh was awakened by the phone ringing downstairs. He looked at the clock. It was 6:00 am. He could faintly hear Aunt Lo speaking to someone, but he couldn't make out what she was saying, her voice sounded muffled. After a moment her voice stopped, and Josh figured she had hung up the phone. He got out of bed, dressed quickly, put on his boots, and made his way down the stairs. He found Aunt Lo sitting at the kitchen table. He said, "Who was on the phone?"

"Sit down, Josh." He did as she asked. She said, "It was the hospital. Woody passed away this morning."

In anger, Josh slammed his fists down on the table. The table shook and the salt and pepper shakers rattled. He stood quickly. "Goddamit," he shouted and bolted toward the door. He ran down the steps and into the shop. Before she could stop him, Lo shouted, "Josh! Wait!"

He didn't stop. He climbed on his bike, started the engine, and without his helmet on, placed the bike in gear and raced out of the shop and onto the road toward town at a very high rate of speed.

* * *

The telephone rang at the Fisher residence at 6:20. Dan and Lisa were seated at the table eating breakfast. Nancy answered the phone in the kitchen. Dan and Lisa heard one side of the conversation. Nancy said into the phone, "Hello"

She listened for a moment and said, "Aw, Lo. I'm so sorry."

Hearing her say that caught Dan and Lisa's attention.

Silence while Nancy listened. Then she said into the phone, "Okay. I'll call you right away if he shows up here." Then she hung up the phone.

Nancy turned to face Dan and Lisa, and she said, "Woody died early this morning."

"Oh, no," Lisa said.

Nancy continued, "When Lo told Josh, he stormed out of the house, got on his bike, and was heading toward town... very fast. She asked me to call her if he showed up here."

"Damn," Dan said. "How long ago did he leave?"

"She didn't say but probably no more than a few minutes ago.", Nancy replied.

Just then Lisa heard Josh's motorcycle coming up the street. She got up and ran to the door shouting "he's here".

She ran out the door just as Josh was pulling up to the curb. He placed the kickstand down, shut the engine off, and climbed off the bike. He was greeted immediately by Lisa who wrapped her arms around him. He said, "Uncle Woody died."

Lisa said, "I know. Lo just called."

"I don't know what to do. I can't fix this." He said

"Come in the house," Lisa said. "I'll tell you what you're going to do."

They walked into the house and were greeted by Nancy and Dan. Nancy ran to him and hugged him. She said, "I'm so sorry, Josh"

Dan echoed his wife's sentiment.

Lisa led Josh into the den. Nancy and Dan followed. Nancy said, "I called Lo, she was worried about you. I told her you were here."

Josh simply nodded his head.

Lisa said, "I'm taking you home. Right now. Lo needs you." She said, "Daddy, would you look after Josh's bike?"

Dan said, "Absolutely."

Lisa grabbed her car keys and told Josh, "Let's go."

On their way back to the farm, Lisa said. "Here's what you need to do. You need to apologize to Lo for running off like you did. You probably scared the shit out of her."

Josh said, "I know. I'm sorry."

Lisa being as stern as she had ever been said, "Don't apologize to me. Apologize to your Aunt Lo. She's the one who's earned it."

"I know you're right. I just lost my head."

Lisa said, "Baby, I love you more than anything and I'll do anything for you. If that means coming down hard on you sometimes then that's exactly what I'll do. I don't mean to be a bitch; I'm doing this for your benefit. Understand?"

Josh nodded and said, "Yeah. Thank you."

"I know it's hard, but you will get through this. I promise."

* * *

Lo was seated at the kitchen table looking out the window when she saw Lisa's car pull into the yard. She got up and ran out the front door and down the porch steps and wrapped her loving arms around Josh as soon as he exited the car. She said in his ear, "You scared the hell out of me. Don't ever do that again."

Josh said, "I know. I'm sorry I ran off like I did. I promise I won't ever do it again."

Lo broke off the hug and placed her hands on both sides of Josh's face. Looking him squarely in the eye she said, "I mean it. Don't ever scare me like that again. I need you. Understand?"

Josh said, "Yes, Ma'am" and Lo hugged him again with tears running down her face. She glanced over at Lisa who was standing in front of her car watching. Lisa was crying too when Lo motioned for her to join her, and Josh. Lisa went to them quickly and wrapped her arms around them both.

Thirty minutes later, the three of them were sitting at the kitchen table. Josh, in his usual chair, was staring blankly down at the table, deep in thought. Lisa and Lo were talking but Josh was paying no attention to them. Finally, Lo said, "Josh." No answer. Lo, more loudly said, "Joshua!"

Josh snapped his head up when he heard his full name.

"Are you alright?", Lo asked. "What are you thinking about?"

Josh said, "I was just sitting here thinking about all the conversations we've had at this table. Uncle Woody told me what the plan for the day would be. Talking about our days during dinner. The laughter. The amazing meals you always made for us. All of it."

Lisa and Lo looked at each other sadly. Lo said, "We did have some good times here, didn't we, Buddy?"

Josh nodded, 'yes'

Lo said, "I need to go to the mortuary and discuss Woody's funeral with the funeral director and take Woody's suit to him. Then we need to go to the men's store in town and get you a new suit for the funeral."

Lisa said, "I'd be happy to take him. I've always wanted to dress him up."

That got a chuckle out of Lo and even Josh.

Lo said, "That would be great. It'll be good for you to get out of the house for a little while, Josh."

Josh nodded again and said, "I have to call Emily first." and resumed staring at the table.

* * *

The obituary for Woodrow Bailey read:

Woodrow 'Woody' Alan Bailey (56) passed away on May 19th, 1989, following a brief fight with cancer.

He was born on January 7th, 1933.

Upon graduation from Anthony High School in 1951, he joined the United States Army and served honorably during the Korean War for which he was awarded the Bronze Star.

After his term of service, Woody returned to Anthony and married Loanne Gayle Briggs in 1953.

Woody was active within the community and known for his generosity and integrity.

In 1982, he and his wife adopted their nephew, Joshua Bailey whom they raised as their own.

He is survived by his wife Loanne Bailey of Anthony, his niece Emily Baker of St. Joseph, Missouri, and his nephew, Joshua Bailey of Anthony.

There will be a viewing at Campbell's Funeral home on May 25th from 6:00 to 8:00.

The funeral service will be held at the First Christian Church of Anthony on May 26th at 10:00 a.m. followed by a luncheon provided by the church in the fellowship hall at that location.

Graveside service will be held at Fort Scott National Cemetery in Ft. Scott, Kansas on May 27th at 11:00 a.m.

* * *

Loanne wrote and submitted the obituary to the local newspaper in Anthony as well as the Wichita Eagle. Due to Woody's popularity, it was decided to have his funeral at the church so more people could attend. The chapel at the funeral home would not be large enough to hold the many mourners that were expected.

* * *

On the day before the funeral, Josh was busying himself in the shop when he heard a car pull up to the house. He looked around the corner of the large shop door and saw two men get out of a black sedan. Upon closer examination, he noticed the car had Virginia plates on it. The two men walked up the steps to the front porch. They were both dressed casually, wearing dark slacks with simple button-down shirts and sports jackets. Both men appeared to be in their early 60s with graying, short neatly trimmed hair. One was a few inches taller than the other. The taller man had a gray mustache and the other was clean-shaven. As they walked toward the porch, Josh noticed they both had the same type of stride. Purposeful and precise. They rang the doorbell, and Josh went about continuing his work. He was washing his bike. Mostly to keep himself busy. The day's farm chores had been completed that morning, but he was restless, and washing his bike was a good distraction.

Several minutes later, Aunt Lo walked into the shop and said, "Josh, honey, there are two men here to see you."

"I saw them pull in." Josh said, "What do they want?"

Lo replied, "They're both former soldiers who fought with Woody in Korea."

"Do you know them?" Josh asked.

"I do," Lo replied. "I've known them for a long time but

haven't seen them in years. They were at mine and Woody's wedding. They would like to have a word with you."

Josh walked into the house behind Lo, and she introduced them to Josh. The tall one's name was George Smith and the other's name was Frank Olsen. They had been seated in the living room and when Josh walked in, both men stood to shake Josh's hand. The taller one said, "Josh, my name is George Smith as Loanne mentioned and this is Frank Olsen."

Josh shook their hands, and Lo asked them to be seated. She said, "I have a few things to do, I'll leave you alone so you can talk."

The shorter man spoke, "We were sorry to hear about your Uncle Woody. We served with him in Korea and wanted to come out and express our condolences."

Josh said, "Thanks. I appreciate it."

The two men glanced at each other and the taller one, George said. "Your Uncle Woody told us a lot about you. We've stayed in contact since our departure from the Army. He spoke very highly of you."

Josh sat still in silence…listening.

The man named Frank said, "Woody told us that you are smart and that you're good with a rifle."

Josh had an uneasy feeling as to where this conversation was going. He said, "I had the best teacher."

George said, "No doubt. If Woody taught you, you did, in fact, have the best."

Frank said, "What did your uncle tell you about his time in Korea?"

Josh said, "Honestly, I'm not comfortable discussing what he told me. I don't know you two and I am very secretive."

George said, "Let me guess. He told you that he was a sniper and that he was very good. He also told you that he had over ten confirmed kills during the war."

Josh said nothing.

Frank said, "Joshua, we're here for an additional reason. It's true we are here for your uncle's funeral tomorrow, but we are also here to get to know you a little better." He continued. "Your uncle told us that not only are you good with a rifle but you're also good with your hands and can handle yourself in a fight."

Josh said, "Let me stop you right there. If you're attempting to recruit me into the Army, it won't happen. I have a responsibility to Aunt Lo, and I have a girlfriend who I intend to marry someday. Joining the service is not part of my plan."

George said, "We are not here to try to recruit you into the Army. We have something else in mind."

Josh said, "My Uncle Woody told me many times that I don't need to go looking for trouble, it'll find me soon enough. No disrespect intended, but looking at you two gentlemen I sense trouble."

The two men smiled at each other. Frank said to George, "Yep. Woody trained him alright."

Josh said, "Did I say something funny?"

"Not at all," George said. "It's just that you sound just like your uncle."

"What is it that you want then?" Josh asked.

Frank answered, "We have an organization that helps people who are seeking justice when the courts fail them. We understand from Woody that you've had a similar experience."

Josh began to grimace. "You might say that.".

George said, "We would like to call on you to assist us from time to time."

Josh said, "You've already pointed out that I'm good with a rifle and good with my hands. That indicates to me that you're looking for an assassin. Someone to do the dirty work that the judges and law enforcement are unable to do. Does that sound accurate?"

Frank and George looked at each other knowingly and Frank said, "Woody did say the kid was smart. He was right."

Josh said, "I appreciate what you're trying to do and perhaps some other time in the future. Right now, I'm focused on taking care of the farm and my Aunt Lo as well as taking care of my girlfriend. Nothing, and I mean nothing will prevent me from doing those things. Thank you for coming all the way from Virginia to see us and for attending Uncle Woody's funeral tomorrow. We both appreciate it, but for now, I'm going to have to decline your offer."

Both men stood and George reached into his jacket pocket and retrieved a business card. It was black with white numbers on it. No name, no address, just a phone number. George handed the card to Josh and said, "If you change your mind. Here's my card. Again, our deepest condolences to you and your aunt."

"Thank you," Josh said.

Frank said, "Woody was a good man and a good soldier. He saved our lives more than once. I just thought you might want to know that."

"He certainly was the best man I've ever known. He saved my life too." Josh said.

The two men walked to the door and Frank said, "Give your aunt our best and tell her we'll see her tomorrow."

"I will". Josh said.

Josh watched the two men walk down the steps of the front porch get into their car and drive away. He looked down at the business card and said out loud to himself. "Trouble has found me again."

* * *

Aunt Lo came into the kitchen where she found Josh sitting in his usual spot at the kitchen table. He was staring at the card the men gave him.

She asked, "What did you tell them?"

Josh looked up at her and said, "You know why they were here?"

"Woody told me before he died that they would be here," Lo said.

"So, you know what they wanted and what they do?"

"I do. What did you tell them?"

"I told them I'm not interested at this time. I told them that my responsibility is with you and Lisa, and I declined their offer."

"I see", Lo said. "That's fine. Maybe someday you'll change your mind. Remember, Woody recommended you to them. He had full faith in your skills. It was his idea, but he also expected you to decline their offer until a later time. I know Woody asked you to take care of me and I'm glad you are. At some point, though, you'll need to move on to something more beneficial. It may be years from now, but it will happen."

* * *

That evening at the funeral home, Josh and Lo greeted many people who had come for Woody's viewing. Josh knew most of them and although he was uncomfortable with it, he pushed through for Lo and Woody.

The chapel was small. It reminded Josh of his mother's funeral except this time there were many more flower bouquets which filled the room with the aroma of the fresh cut flowers all with cards attached. Just like with his mother's death, the chapel had sad organ music playing softly from speakers in the ceiling. At the back of the chapel, there was a table with framed photographs of Woody that Lo had set up. Two were photos of his time in Korea. Josh looked closely at them and recognized the two men who had visited him earlier in the day. They were much younger in the pictures, but Josh recognized them easily. The other photographs were mostly of Woody and Lo. A few from their wedding and others from over the years. There were a couple of them with Dan and Nancy Fisher. In one of them, Dan was holding a child and Nancy holding another. Josh smiled when he realized that the child Dan was holding was Lisa. She was two years old then and Nancy was holding Lori who was an infant in the picture. There was another photograph that Josh stood staring at for several minutes. It was a photo of himself and Woody standing in front of their bikes. He remembered that Lo had taken it on his sixteenth birthday.

They were both smiling big with their arms around each other's shoulders. He was still looking intently at the photograph when someone tapped him on the shoulder. He turned and there stood Lance and Becky. He smiled immediately and gave his friend a big hug and then Becky. He said, "I'm so happy to see you two. Thank you so much for coming."

Lance said, "We wouldn't miss it. I always liked Woody. Besides, your aunt Lo asked me to be a pallbearer."

Josh said, "She did? I had no idea."

"I think she wanted it to be a surprise," Lance said.

"Well then, she succeeded. That's terrific. Thanks, for doing that."

Lance said, "No need to thank me. It's an honor."

"He was very fond of you, Buddy. He didn't care much for your long hair, but you always seemed to make him laugh. Not many folks could do that"

Becky said, "How are you holding up?"

"I'm doing pretty well," Josh said. "Lisa has been amazing throughout this whole thing. She keeps me focused and doesn't allow me to get too down." He continued, "How are you doing?"

Becky said, "We're doing great. Where is Lisa?"

"She'll be here soon. She's coming with Dan, Nancy, and Lori."

Lance said, "We're going to go pay our respects to Woody. We'll talk to you later."

Josh nodded and said, "Thanks again for being here. It means a lot to me."

Josh watched them walk over to Aunt Lo, give her a hug,

and walk slowly down the aisle to where Woody's coffin lay open.

The number of mourners increased as the evening wore on. So many people wanted to show their respect. It made Josh feel proud and it warmed his heart to see so much respect being given to his uncle. Woody most certainly had earned it. Josh and Lo would walk down to look at Woody from time to time. Once more people arrived, they allowed them space to visit Woody and not get in anyone's way.

The Fisher family arrived, and they all exchanged hugs and the Fisher's expressed their condolences. Lo and Josh thanked them profusely for all their help and generosity over the past few months. Lisa hugged Josh and Josh said, "Lance and Becky are here. They're sitting about halfway down on the right."

Lisa quickly moved down the aisle. Josh watched with a smile on his face the three friends hugging and smiling at seeing each other. Lisa sat with them for a few minutes while Josh continued to greet folks coming into the chapel.

Lo said, "Josh, look who's here."

Josh turned and saw Emily walking through the opened double doors. She had her hair tied back and was wearing all black. Emily came to him quickly, grabbed him tightly, and said, "I'm so sorry for your loss."

Josh said, "I wish you could have gotten to know him better. I'm sorry you couldn't."

"It's okay," She said, "I'm happy I got to meet him. In the very short time I knew him, I could tell he was a good man and more importantly, he took wonderful care of my little brother."

"That he did," Josh said. "Where's Jessica?"

"She had to stay in St. Joe. She's minding the bar and steakhouse while I'm here. She sends her best and said she's keeping you all in her thoughts."

Lo came over and hugged Emily and thanked her for being there. She told Emily that she would like her to sit with them at the funeral the next day. She insisted. Emily agreed and she walked down to visit Woody. When she finished and walked back to find a seat, Lisa noticed her and jumped up to hug her and say 'hello'. She then introduced Emily to Lance and Becky.

Lance said, "So you're the big sister?"

Emily smiled and said, "I certainly am."

Lance said with a smile. "We've heard a lot about you. All of it is good. It's an honor to meet the big sister of my best friend."

Becky nodded her agreement and said, "Your brother is one of a kind. A hero to nearly everyone here. We love him very much."

Emily said, "That's quite a remarkable statement. Thank you."

When everyone left, Josh, Lo, Emily, and Lisa took one last walk down the aisle to see Woody. Lo and Josh said goodnight to Woody, and they would see him tomorrow. Josh asked if Lo needed anything else and she replied, "No".

He said, "We're going to meet Lance and Becky at Pizza

Hut and talk for a while. We're kidnapping Emily and taking her with us. Besides, we want a ride in Em's badass Camaro."

Emily said, "Absolutely."

Lo said to Emily, "And you're staying with us tonight too."

Emily said she would.

* * *

They were all sitting at a long table in Pizza Hut. The mood was pleasant. There was no talk of funerals or cancer or anything remotely depressing. Lance and Becky had fun telling stories to Emily about Josh when he was a kid. There was plenty of laughter at Pizza Hut that night.

CHAPTER 13

"You look so handsome," Lo said when Josh walked into the kitchen. "Lisa did a great job picking out your suit."

Josh shrugged. He was wearing the dark suit that Lisa had chosen for him last week. It fit him perfectly. His short brown hair had just a slight hint of gel in it. His 5'7" frame stood straight. He had on a new pair of black dress shoes.

Emily looked up from her breakfast and said, "Wow. You look amazing, little brother."

She had already been up and dressed nicely in an all-black sheath. She had simple studs in her ears and her soft, brown hair hung perfectly on her shoulders.

Lo was also dressed in black with simple earrings. Nothing too gaudy or pretentious. Her gorgeous black hair was tied up neatly and her makeup was perfect.

They talked a little about what would happen today. Lo told them that at some point during the funeral, people would be asked if they wanted to speak. Josh said he would like to say something if that was right. Lo told him he was most certainly welcome to.

* * *

The town of Anthony was, for the most part, completely closed. Most stores in town had signs on their doors and windows that stated, 'Closed for funeral'.

When they arrived at the church, they noticed that the hearse was parked outside. They went inside and entered the sanctuary; they saw Woody's coffin resting in front of the pulpit that was on the stage. It was open and an American flag was draped appropriately across the bottom. The many bouquets of flowers surrounded the coffin and there were four large, framed photographs as well. The one just above Woody was his official Army photo from when he was a recruit. Next to that was another large photograph of Woody and Lo taken at their wedding. On the right side was a photograph of Woody and Lo taken more recently and on the opposite side was a large photo of Woody, Lo, and Josh that Dan Fisher had taken at Thanksgiving last year.

At the entrance to the sanctuary, stood two soldiers at attention. They were dressed in their perfectly pressed uniforms. Faces forward and stern. Perfectly still. A few people had already arrived and had seated themselves in pews.

It wasn't long before the sanctuary was filled with mourners. Josh and Lo had tried to greet all of them as they entered but there were so many, it was impossible to thank all of them for coming. When the Fishers arrived, Lisa stayed with Josh, not once leaving his side where she would remain mostly the entire day. She was dressed in a simple unassuming black dress. The bottom was just above her knees showing just enough leg to be deemed appropriate. Her blonde hair was tied neatly back. Becky found a seat near the front while Lance would be sitting with the other pallbearers. One of whom was, of course, Dan Fisher.

Once it was felt that all the guests had arrived. Lo, Josh, Emily, and Lisa made their way slowly down the aisle. It had been decided by Aunt Lo several days before that Lisa would join them and sit with them. When they approached Woody's coffin, they all looked at Woody and said their goodbyes. Lo kissed her fingers and then touched them to Woody's forehead. Josh had secretly brought with him Woody's favorite John Deere cap and laid it on Woody's crossed hands. Lo saw him and had to smile. They took their seats with Lo sitting next to the aisle with Josh next to her. Lisa sat next to Josh and Emily was on Lisa's other side.

The organist was playing hymns that Josh didn't recognize but felt were appropriate. Then from the back of the sanctuary, they could hear one of the soldiers speaking softly and stating orders to the other. They both marched in perfect step slowly and methodically to the front of the sanctuary. They then each turned sharply. One toward the foot of the coffin, the other to the head. The lead soldier gently lowered the lid of the coffin covering Woody's face, then with precision, grabbed the flag and draped it slowly across the remaining uncovered portion of the coffin. The blue field with stars lay across the head of the coffin. Each soldier adjusted the flag until it rested perfectly square over Woody's coffin. When they had completed that task, each of them rendered a slow four-count salute, held the salute for three seconds then slowly lowered their hand back to their sides. The lead soldier quietly stated another order and the two met in front of the coffin and then marched in step to the back of the sanctuary where they would remain at attention for the remainder of the funeral.

The pastor rose and spoke. He welcomed everyone and then read the obituary that Lo had written verbatim. He then introduced Dan and Dan walked up to the pulpit. Dan spoke of his friend and told a couple of humorous stories to help lighten the mood a bit. He also told of Woody's generosity and integrity. He talked about how his friend of many years would help those in need, never asking for anything in return. Dan then finished his eulogy by saying, "Goodbye my friend. I will miss you."

The pastor stood again and asked if anyone else would like to share a story. No one stood. Josh believed they felt as though they couldn't top Dan's eulogy and didn't need to. Finally, after realizing no one else would speak, Josh squeezed Lo's hand, stood made his way up the two steps, and placed himself at the pulpit. There was a box of tissues resting on the pulpit and a microphone sticking up from in front of it. He looked out at the overwhelming number of people there, then he looked at his Aunt Lo, Lisa, and Emily. Lisa, holding onto Lo's hand winked at him and gave him a look of assurance. He felt her gaze and knew she was telling him he would do great. He took a deep breath and spoke. He was determined to get through this with dignity.

"First, on behalf of Aunt Lo, Emily, and myself, I want to

thank all of you for being here today." He continued, "When I was twelve years old, I lost my mother suddenly." He glanced at Lisa and Lo, and they were shaking their heads back and forth slightly. He continued, "When she died, I had no family, nowhere to go, and no idea what my future would be like." Lo let out a small sigh of relief. He said, "About two weeks after my mother died, this couple who I didn't know arrived at the home where I was staying while awaiting my future. That couple was my Uncle Woody and Aunt Lo. To make a long story short, they gained custody of me, brought me here to this wonderful town, and raised me as their own." He was fighting back tears at the memory he was sharing with the world. "Uncle Woody and Aunt Loanne saved my life. If it wasn't for them, I would most likely be in prison or worse. Uncle Woody taught me many things. He taught me how to drive a pickup, tractors, combines. He taught me how to ride a motorcycle. Which, incidentally, I know that my girlfriend, Lisa, appreciates very much." That got a small chuckle out of the attentive crowd. "But what Uncle Woody did for me the most was what he taught me through example. Simply by watching him and listening to him, I've learned so many more important things. Things like integrity, the importance of hard work, and honesty. He taught me the value of being a good man and caring about humanity. He taught me the importance of protecting those who cannot protect themselves and to do it altruistically. He taught me that it's okay to make mistakes if I own them and apologize genuinely for them." He paused because he was unable to hold back the tears any longer. He grabbed a tissue and dabbed it at his eyes. He continued. "I told myself I would get through this." He chuckled slightly. "I owe my uncle my life. He and Aunt Lo have made me who I am today." He sniffed hard. "That's why I am speaking to you now. Because I owe him."

Josh looked out at the crowd for just a second then bent his head down looking at Woody's flag-draped coffin before him. He said, stating the words through tears and gasps, "Thank you, Uncle Woody, for saving me and teaching me and protecting me. You were...the only father figure...I ever had...and I couldn't be more blessed. It is my goal in life to make you proud of me. I love you and I miss you so much."

Josh walked off the stage while Lo stood, and he went directly into Lo's waiting arms.

There wasn't a dry eye in the entire sanctuary.

At the back of the sanctuary, a person who Josh did not know played 'Amazing Grace' on the bagpipes. Everyone sat solemnly while he played. Lo, Josh, Lisa, and Emily all held hands. When the song was finished, the Pastor came up to the pulpit, said a prayer, and then announced that a luncheon was being served immediately following the service. He then said that the graveside service would be the next day at Fort Scott National Cemetery at 11:00 a.m.

The basement at the church was filled with large round tables and decorated with nice, white linen tablecloths. There were flowers at the center of each table. The ladies of the church had made many different items to eat. Attendees of the funeral all waited patiently in line to fill their plates with an assortment of food. The chatter among people was somewhat lively. People were telling Woody stories at their tables. Occasionally a table of folks would erupt with laughter.

Josh, Lo, Lisa, and Emily were seated at a long table off to the side. As people finished eating and began to depart, many of them stopped at their tables to express their condolences. Some of them thanked Josh for his eulogy. Nancy Fisher even went so far as to tell Josh, "That was the most heartwarming eulogy I've ever heard. Woody would have been so proud of you today."

Once most of the guests left, Lance and Becky caught up with Lisa and Josh who were standing and greeting people as they walked out.

Lance said, "Before we go, we have something to tell you. My band is playing our first gig at Pogo's in Wichita next Friday. We'd love it if you two could be there."

Lisa said, "We wouldn't miss it for the world."

Josh nodded his agreement.

Becky said, "They're opening for another band. When they finish, we want you guys to stay the night with us if you can."

Josh and Lisa said they'd love that.

Josh asked Lance, "Are you going to make it to Ft. Scott tomorrow?"

Lance said, "Of course."

They said their goodbyes. Lance and Becky wanted to spend the rest of the day visiting their parents and they would see them tomorrow.

* * *

It had been decided before the funeral that there would be a caravan driving to Ft. Scott for Woody's interment. All in all, there were six vehicles that made the trip. They all met at Fisher's farm store at 6:00 a.m. and made the four-hour trip to Fort Scott. Emily drove her Camaro; she would be heading back to St. Joseph following the service. Lance and Becky had their own car. They would need to return to Wichita. Dan and Nancy drove their own car as well while the other pallbearers and their spouses drove in vans and other shared conveyances. A few days before, Josh told Lo that he would like to use her Cadillac to take Lisa to Pleasanton. He wanted to see a couple of people and visit his mom's gravesite. Lo told him that would be fine, and that she would ride back to Anthony with Dan and Nancy after the service.

Fort Scott National Cemetery no.1 sat on a hill. It had been established in the 1800s and had 800 military members buried there. There was a large gate at the entrance and the grounds were impeccably maintained. When the convoy arrived, they found the hearse parked and waiting. There were several soldiers standing by. There was a covered area that was used for services. It had a wheeled cart sitting in the middle of it waiting for Woody's coffin to be placed on it for the service. The burial itself would take place later in the day and would be handled by the military. The pallbearers walked to the back of the hearse and were given instructions on what to do and where to go with the coffin. Josh, Lisa, and Emily made their way to the seating area along with other mourners. When they got to the pavilion, a very kind Army Chaplain greeted them and instructed them on where they would be sitting. Lo would be in the first chair to the left then Josh, Lisa, and Emily. The door to the hearse was opened by the funeral director and the coffin was gingerly pulled out a couple of feet. Following the previous instructions, the pallbearers gently grabbed the coffin and made the short walk to the pavilion where they softly laid Woody's coffin on the wheeled cart. 50 feet off to the side were three soldiers with rifles standing at attention. Beyond them, another 30 feet stood a soldier with a bugle in her hand also at attention. The two soldiers that were at the funeral the day before marched to Woody's coffin and they checked the flag to be sure it was placed perfectly on the coffin. When they finished and marched away, the Chaplain greeted everyone, said a prayer, and recited Woody's obituary just as the preacher had done twenty-four hours before. He said a few kind words and when he finished, he took a few steps back.

The United States military takes graveside services and funerals of their fallen very seriously. Everything must be done perfectly. Every action and movement is choreographed. Respect and dignity are the rules. First and foremost.

The two soldiers marched to the coffin, split and one went to the foot and the other to the head of the coffin. They each gave a salute to the flag and then proceeded to lift the flag gently from the coffin with white-gloved hands. They each held their ends of the flag and sidestepped three steps from the coffin. They folded the flag in half then turned it and folded it in half again. Each soldier is in perfect orchestration with the other. Every movement by the soldiers was precise and deliberate. With the flag quartered they stretched it out, so it was taught. The soldier with the striped end of the flag began to fold the flag creating a triangle. With each fold, he would be sure there were no wrinkles of any kind. It was clear they had practiced this art many times.

When they had completed the triangle, The lead soldier turned the flag, so it was flat in his hands. One hand on top and the other directly underneath the flag. He slowly and deliberately marched to where Loanne was seated. He spun the flag, so the point of the triangle faced him. He bent down to Lo and said, "On behalf of the president of the United States, The United States Army, and a grateful nation, please accept this flag as a symbol of our appreciation for your loved one's honorable and faithful service"

Lo accepted the flag and said, "Thank you", and laid the flag on her lap. The soldier then raised up, took one step back, and did a slow four-count salute holding it for three seconds and slowly putting his arm back to his side just like they had done at Woody's funeral the day before.

Over where the three soldiers were waiting with rifles, a command was given. Josh was pretty sure he said, "Present arms." The soldiers snapped their rifles up and the command 'FIRE' was shouted. The first volley took some of the guests by surprise, some of them jumped at the sound of the crack. Then another command and another volley, then a third. The soldiers immediately got back to attention and the bugler began playing. All soldiers saluted while the bugler played.

It was an experience Josh would never forget. His chest swelled with pride over the amount of respect the military gave his Uncle Woody. Tears were falling down Lo's cheeks as they listened to the somber playing of 'Taps'.

* * *

The guests made their way back to their vehicles. Lo thanked everyone for coming so far and for their generosity. Many hugs were given and received. Lance and Becky hugged Josh and Lisa and said they would see them next weekend. Emily hugged Lo then Lisa and then Josh. She whispered in his ear. "Please take care of yourself. Let me hear from you when you get home."

Josh said he would call when he got home and said 'goodbye'.

Dan walked over to Josh and shook his hand. He said, "Woody would have been so proud of you right now."

Josh said, "Thank you."

Then Dan said, "We're proud of you too. You're a good man, Josh. Nancy and I are very happy with the way you treat our daughter."

Josh told him, "It's my honor, sir."

Dan and Nancy got into their car while Lisa got in the passenger seat of Lo's Cadillac. Lo and Josh stood looking at each other and then hugged tightly. She said, "Please be careful and come home safe to me."

Josh said, "I will. I promise."

Then Lo said with a smile, "And take good care of my Caddy."

* * *

The drive to Pleasanton was only thirty minutes long. Lisa and Josh talked about the service and how respectful it was. They discussed their plan to meet up with Lance and Becky next weekend. They were both looking forward to it.

As they got closer to Pleasanton, Josh began to focus on what they were going to do there. Lisa asked, "Are we going to visit your mom?"

Josh replied, "If that's okay."

Lisa said, "Of course it is. We're a team. What affects you affects me."

Josh said, "We're also going to visit a couple of people. One, who I want you to meet in particular. I just hope I can remember where everything is."

They pulled into town and Josh's memory was beginning to come back to him. They made their way downtown and Josh pulled the Caddy in front of the Sheriff's office. They got out and walked inside. When Josh entered the building, he noticed the same lady that was there seven years ago. Phyllis looked up at him and asked, "May I help you."

Josh said, "I'd like to speak to Sheriff Hilts if I could, please."

Phyllis asked his name and Josh said, "I'm Joshua Bailey"

Her eyes lit up and a big smile crossed her face, "Oh my," She exclaimed, "Sheriff Hilts will definitely want to see you."

She picked up her phone tapped a couple of buttons and said into the phone while winking at Josh, "There's a Joshua Bailey here to see you."

Josh could hear the voice on the other end shout, "I'll be right there"

Within seconds, Sheriff Hilts came down the hallway and

reached out his hand to shake Josh's. He said, "Josh Bailey. It's good to see you. Come on back to my office." He told Phyllis, "Hold all calls unless it's an emergency."

The three of them entered Hilts' office and took seats. Josh looked around the office. Josh said, "So you're the Sheriff now?"

Hilts smiled and said, "Two years. How have you been?"

Josh said he was good and introduced him to Lisa.

"What brings you back here?" Hilts asked.

Josh said, "We just left the funeral for my uncle in Fort Scott and decided to come up here. I wanted to thank you for how you treated me the night my mom died. I don't think I ever did that properly."

Hilts said, "I'm sorry to hear about your uncle. I appreciate you stopping in. I've wondered about you many times over the years. It's good to know you're doing well."

Josh said, "I hear you met my sister."

"Oh, man," Hilts said, "That was quite a shock. So, I guess she found you."

Josh said jokingly, "Can't put anything past you, huh? It's a good thing you're in law enforcement."

Lisa giggled and Hilts laughed.

Josh asked, "Is Pastor Stevens still around?"

"He is," Hilts said, "Boy is he going to be surprised to see you. I hope you don't give him a heart attack when you show up at his door."

"My sister said he's retired."

"Yeah, but he's still kicking around town." Hilts said, "I see him once in a while."

Josh said, "Well, we just wanted to stop in and say hello.

Thanks again for the way you handled things when my mom died. I want you to know that I haven't forgotten about it."

"Don't mention it." Hilts said, "I'm so glad you came by. It really made my day. Take care of yourself and again, I'm glad things turned out well for you."

* * *

The drive to Pastor Stevens' house was easier than Josh thought it would be. While many things had changed over the past seven years, he was happy that he could remember his way around.

They pulled up in front of the Pastor's home. Josh looked at it for a moment. He said to Lisa, "This is where I stayed after mom died. It was here where I met Uncle Woody and Aunt Lo for the first time."

Lisa nodded. "Are you alright?"

Josh said, "I'm fine. I'm way overdue with this visit."

They walked up the sidewalk to the front porch, rang the doorbell, and waited. It only took a couple of seconds until the door opened. Pastor Stevens stood with the door open, and Josh said, "Pastor Stevens? It's good to see you. I'm Josh Bailey and this is my girlfriend, Lisa."

Pastor Stevens smiled even bigger than Phyllis did at the police station. He said, "Well bless your heart, Josh. Come on in. It's so good to see you."

They went into the house and into the living room. Pastor Stevens while sitting said, "I've wondered about you so many times over the years. How long has it been?"

"Seven years," Josh replied.

"My memory is beginning to fade. I met your sister. Was she able to find you.?"

"Thanks to you, yes. She said you told her where to look and you were right."

"That's wonderful, Josh." Pastor Stevens continued. "How have you been?"

Josh told him about growing up on the farm and that Lo and Woody took very good care of him. He made friends quickly and learned so much working on the farm. He told him that he met Lisa on his first day of school. "I've had a very good life since I left here."

"That's terrific, Josh, it warms my heart to hear that." Pastor Stevens couldn't stop smiling.

Josh said, "My uncle Woody died a week or so ago and we had his burial in Fort Scott, so we decided to come up and visit. We've already been to see Sheriff Holts and we're going to visit my mom's grave when we leave here."

Pastor Stevens said, "I'm so sorry to hear about your uncle. As I recall, I got a good sense about him and your aunt."

"They're both wonderful people. I was lucky." Josh continued, "I wanted to tell you thank you for all you did for me when my mom died. You and your wife treated me very well and I don't think that I thanked you properly. I want you to know that I haven't forgotten what you did for me, and I appreciate it." Josh turned to face Lisa and said, "This is the man who wrote my mom's obituary which in turn, caused Uncle Woody and Aunt Lo to find me. If it wasn't for him, I never would have met them or you or Lance or anyone else. My life could have been much worse if it wasn't for this man right here."

Lisa said to Pastor Stevens, "Then I owe you a 'thank you' as well."

Pastor Stevens said, "Just seeing you happy is all the thanks I need, Josh. I'm so very happy for you."

* * *

As they drove to the cemetery, Josh explained a few things to Lisa. He said, "The day Aunt Lo and Uncle Woody and I left, we stopped at the cemetery so I could say 'goodbye' to my mom. At the time her headstone was a flat piece of metal that had her name, date of birth, and her date of death inscribed on it. On that day I made a promise to her that someday I would replace her headstone with a larger one. A few months ago, I ordered a new one and today will be the first time I get to see it."

"Aww. That's so sweet.", Lisa said.

"When we get there, I'm going to talk to her. I don't want you to think I'm crazy."

"I understand," Lisa replied.

They pulled into the cemetery and Josh remembered where his mom's burial site was. They got out of the car and walked hand-in-hand, making their way to his mom's grave. When Josh saw the new headstone, he smiled and said, "There it is."

They stood several feet away from it. The headstone was 3 feet wide and 2 ½ feet tall. It was made of gray granite like most of the other stones in the cemetary. In each of the upper corners, there were lilies etched into it. Below that was Angel's name, her date of birth as well as her date of death.

Under that were the words 'Gone too soon'. Josh said, "Lilies were my mom's favorite flowers."

"It's very nice, Josh. You did well." Lisa said.

Josh spoke to his mom. He said, "I'm sorry it's been so long since I was here. I hope you like your new headstone, Mom. I want you to know that I've had a wonderful life with Uncle Woody and Aunt Lo. They did real good raising me and taking care of me." He paused then said, "This is my girlfriend, Lisa. She was the first person I met when I got to Anthony. Isn't she beautiful? I gave your necklace to her. I hope that was alright." He took a deep breath and said, "I've tried very hard to make you proud of me, Mom."

Just then a bluejay fluttered its way down and landed on top of Angel's new headstone. Josh and Lisa stood stunned and still. The beautiful blue bird looked back and forth between them and chirped for several seconds. Josh and Lisa looked at each other in amazement then back at the bluejay. It chirped again and then suddenly flew away.

* * *

As they drove out of town, Lisa said, "So are we going to talk about what happened? The bluejay?"

Josh said, "That was pretty freaky."

"Do you think it means anything?" Lisa asked.

"Well," Josh replied. "You know I'm not a religious person, but I do believe that things happen sometimes that cannot be explained. Whether it's true or not, my belief is that the Bluejay was carrying the spirit of my mom. She was saying that she was happy to see us and that she was glad I'd had a good life. Do you think I'm nuts for thinking that?"

"Absolutely not," Lisa exclaimed. "I believe the same thing. Just because something may or may not be true doesn't matter. It's how a person feels about it that makes the difference."

"Exactly", Josh said. "No one is harmed by someone else's belief."

CHAPTER 14

A week had passed since Woody's funeral. Josh, Lisa, and Aunt Lo were sitting on the porch watching the wheat sway in the south breeze. Josh said, "How are we going to get all our fields cut? It's just us now."

Lo said, "We may have to hire custom cutters to do most of it. It's expensive but I don't know what else to do."

Josh glanced at Lisa who was sitting with a smile on her face. Josh asked, "What are you smiling about."

Lisa said, "You'll see."

Moments later, several vehicles arrived and pulled into the yard. Josh recognized the first car as Dan and Nancy's car. Then more pulled in. Most were pickups and one right after the other kept coming and coming. All told there were ten vehicles in all. Josh, Lo, and Lisa all stood and moved to the steps as the many farmers climbed out of their cars and trucks. Dan approached them and walked up the steps.

Lo said, "What's going on?"

Dan said, "We're here to help. All these fine folks have volunteered to help get your wheat harvested. All they need from you is a plan and where the locations for all your fields are. Then we'll split them all up and they'll get it done for you."

Lo had a tear coming down her cheek. "That's just about the most amazing gift I think I've ever seen. Thank you all so much."

Josh looked at Lisa and said, "You knew about this didn't you?"

Lisa nodded and said, "Daddy swore me to secrecy."

Lo took all the good Samaritans into the house. She got out her maps and showed everyone where their fields were. Within moments, all the fields to be harvested were assigned and the farmers left.

Later, back in their spots on the porch, Lo said, "You won't find the strength of community better anywhere else."

Josh said, "That's right. How could anyone not want to live among these wonderful people?"

Lo said, "Before you two run off to Wichita for the night, there's something I need to discuss with you. We need to talk about Woody's will. He had it drawn up a long time ago. I get the house, the property, and all the wheat fields. The tractors combine, and all the other equipment. All of it except for a few things that he willed to you." She paused for a second. "Woody wanted you to have the pickup, his rifle and pistol, and...his motorcycle."

Josh was blown away. Part of him was happy but another part of him was sad. "I don't know what to say."

Lo said, "Woody wanted you to have the bike because he

knew how much you love it, and he wanted it to stay in the family. He told me that it was important to him that you keep it and ride it."

"Wow", was all Josh could think of saying.

"There's one more thing," Lo said. "I've decided to sell the farm."

"What?" Josh exclaimed.

"I know you're surprised to hear that, but Woody and I talked it over when we first found out he was sick." She continued. "I told him that I didn't want to stay here and work on the farm without him. It would just be too hard."

Josh thought for a moment, still reeling over this information. He said, "Where will you go? Where will I go?"

"You know the house in town that I told you we rented out? That was the house I grew up in. The current tenant's lease is up in a couple of months. I'm going to move back into my old home. You can come with me and stay as long as you want or until you and Lisa get a place of your own."

More shocking news. Josh said, "Well this has certainly been an informative afternoon, I'll tell you that much."

Lo asked, "Are you upset?"

Josh said, "I made a commitment to you and Uncle Woody. I said I would do whatever you needed. That means supporting any decisions you make. I'm fine with it."

Lisa said, "Yay. You'll only be a couple of blocks from my house."

Lisa stood and said she was going to go get ready for the trip to Wichita. Josh knew from experience that her task would take some time, so he got up and made his way into the shop. When he walked in, he took a deep breath and slowly ambled to where Woody's motorcycle was resting under its cover. Josh delicately removed the tarp and stood back for a moment taking it all in. Then he walked around to the right side of the bike and opened the saddle bag. Inside he saw an assortment of tools. Wrenches, pliers, screwdrivers, some zip ties, and a tire pressure gauge. He closed the bag and went around to the other side and opened the saddle bag on the left. He peered into the bag and saw a plain, white, letter-size envelope with just his name 'Josh' written on it. He opened the envelope and removed the contents. It was a folded sheet of notebook paper. He unfolded it and began to read:

Dear Josh,

If you're reading this then...well, you know.

I wanted to tell you once again how very proud I am of you. You have been a blessing to both me and your Aunt Lo. When we first picked you up, she and I had no idea what we were getting ourselves into. We were both very nervous but determined to give you the best possible life we could. We vowed to protect you, teach you, feed you, and raise you like we would our own son. It is my hope that you feel as though we succeeded.

Please take good care of my motorcycle as I know you will. Ride her often. She'll take good care of you if you take good care of her. It makes me *happy knowing that she'll be taken care of and ridden by you. Remember, you only get one shot at life so make the best of it.*

Love,

Uncle Woody

Josh sighed heavily, folded the note, and placed it back into its envelope, then he folded the envelope and put it in his back pocket.

* * *

Pogo's was a large bar in Wichita that on some nights would allow people under twenty-one to go in. Those who were old enough to drink wore wristbands and those under twenty-one had no band. No wristband; no alcohol. Josh and Lisa entered the cavernous room. It was dark inside with only the stage lights illuminating the room. There were a few pool tables off to the side and some video games. There was a stage and a large dance floor in front of it. They arrived early enough that the bar hadn't filled up yet. Most of the clientele were students who attended Wichita State University. Josh and Lisa made their way down toward the dance floor where they found Becky seated at a table watching Lance and his band getting set up to play. She had reserved a table right in front to get the best view. She turned and saw her two friends approaching, jumped up, and practically ran them over with her excitement at seeing them. She hugged them both and led them to her table. She yelled at Lance who was busying himself with plugging in his guitar to his amp and helping the rest of his bandmates set up their equipment, "Lance," She shouted. "They're here." Lance turned and came walking over to greet them.

Josh said, "Are you nervous? Your first gig and all."

Lance said, "Just excited. Thank you for coming."

Lisa said, "We wouldn't miss this for anything."

* * *

Thirty minutes later, Lance's band began playing. Josh was very impressed with their skill. They played songs from Van Halen, Def Leppard, and even some Led Zeppelin. After each song was over, the crowd cheered. Many of them would dance, including Becky and Lisa. Josh wasn't much of a dancer, but he enjoyed watching Lisa and Becky dancing, smiling, and having a great time. Lisa deserved it after the past few months of dealing with him. He had promised Lisa he would dance at least one slow song with her. When they neared the end of their set, Lance spoke on his microphone, he said, "This next song is dedicated to two of my best friends, Josh and Lisa. It's a song by U2 titled 'With or Without You', we hope you like it. Lisa and Josh, this one's for you."

The band began playing and Lisa grabbed Josh's hand and led him to the dance floor. They wrapped their arms around each other and swayed to the music looking into each other's eyes.

See the stone set in your eyes

See the thorn twist in your side

I'll wait for you

When the song finished, Josh and Lisa kissed and hugged. They looked up at Lance who was grinning from ear to ear. They both mouthed the words 'thank you' and Lance nodded to them 'You're welcome'.

* * *

Later that night, the four friends were sitting in the living room of Lance and Becky's apartment. They laughed and joked until the wee hours of the morning. Finally, Josh said he was tired and thanked Lance and Becky for a fun night. He walked into the spare bedroom where he and Lisa would sleep. Lisa said, "I'll be there in a couple of minutes."

When Josh left the room, Lisa said to Lance and Becky. "Thank you both so much for inviting us. We both needed a night where we could have some fun. Especially Josh. He's had a rough go of it since his Uncle Woody died. He's getting better and tonight I saw a sparkle in his eyes that I haven't seen in a long time. We both owe that to you two."

Lance said, "We're glad you could be here. We miss you guys."

* * *

The next two months were a busy time for Lo and Josh. With the help of their neighbors, they were able to get their wheat cut and began the painstaking job of selling everything. Lo had decided to hold an estate sale. Farmers and townsfolk from all over the county and beyond attended the sale. The yard as well as the road in front of the house was packed with pickups. Many of them with trailers attached. When it was all done, all that was left was to pack up furniture, kitchen supplies, and any other items they were keeping and move them to the house in town. When everything had been moved and they were finished with their last of what seemed like 100 loads to take to town, Lo and Josh stood back and took one last look at the house.

Josh said, "So many wonderful memories."

Lo nodded and said, "So many,"

Lo made enough money on the sale plus what Woody had left her in his will that she was able to retire and spend her days working on the old house, gardening, cooking for local charities, and relaxing. Loanne Bailey's childhood home was a two-story home with three bedrooms and two bathrooms. Over the years, Woody and Lo would make renovations to it between tenants. They added a large garage and bought the property next door. They had that house razed and that gave them an extra-large yard to the side of the house.

Josh was in high demand. Dan had put out word at his store that Josh was looking to work as a hired hand on a farm. Every farmer in the area it seemed wanted him. He had his choice of who he would work for. He still enjoyed his alone time in the tractors and working the fields.

* * *

One evening in early October 1989, the phone rang at Lo's house. Josh answered and the female voice on the other end said, "Josh, this is Jessica, Emily's friend."

Josh said, "Hey, how are..." then he stopped and said. "What's wrong? Is she okay? If you're calling and it isn't Emily, then something must be wrong."

"She's hurt." Jessica said, "She was beaten badly last night. She's in the hospital and they had to wire her jaw shut. That's why I'm calling and she's not. She can't speak"

"Shit," Josh exclaimed. "Give me the name and address of the hospital."

Jessica told him the name and the address and gave him directions on how to get there.

Josh said, "Thanks. I'll be there in the morning."

Jessica tried to say, "There's something else..." but Josh had already hung up the phone.

Josh called Lisa and told her about his conversation with Jessica and that he needed to leave right away. Lisa told him to be safe and call her as soon as he arrived. No matter how late it was. And "Give 'em my best."

Lo arrived at the house a few minutes later and Josh told her what happened and that he needed to go to St. Joe. She said, "Just be safe and let me know when you get there. Send my love to Emily and let her know I'm thinking about her."

Josh went out to the garage and grabbed all the items he thought he might need. Then he went to his bedroom and packed three days' worth of clothing. He put everything in the pickup and left.

As he drove, he was already formulating in his mind what he needed to do.

CHAPTER 15

Emily Baker had just closed the bar. She walked outside locked the back door to the steakhouse and took a few steps to her car when she felt a horrific pain in her lower back. Her legs gave out and she went down onto the hard concrete. She felt someone grab the back of her shirt and drag her. Then another bad pain on the right side of her face, breaking her jaw. Then another sharp pain in her left leg. She heard a voice say, "You fucking, bitch. You've turned me down for the last time. If you tell anyone about this, I'll cut your fucking throat."

She recognized the voice instantly; it was Derek Johnson. He punched her hard in her right eye then she heard him run off just before passing out from the pain.

* * *

Josh arrived in St. Joseph a little after 1:00 a.m.

He stopped at a convenience store and used a pay phone in front of the store to call Lisa and tell her that he had made it safe, and that he would call her again in the morning after he saw Emily.

The hospital in St. Joe was five stories tall and made of red brick. It looked as if it had been built in the 50s. He pulled in and drove slowly around the parking lot. He spotted Emily's Camaro and assumed that Jessica had been driving it. He found a spot at the back of the lot where he could see the main entrance. He backed the pickup into its spot, shut the engine off laid down in the seat, and went to sleep.

He woke up a few hours later and checked his watch. It was 6:30 in the morning. He stretched and got out of the pickup, looked around, and walked toward the main entrance of the hospital. Once he got inside, he found a restroom and took care of pertinent business then found the front desk. There was a pleasant-looking lady seated there. He told her he was looking for Emily Baker. She asked if he was family, and he told her that he was her brother. The desk clerk looked up Emily's name in her book, found her room number, and dialed it. He heard her say to someone, "There's someone here to see Emily. He claims to be Emily's brother". She listened to the response and hung up the phone. She said, "Someone will be right down."

Josh drifted away from the receptionist and began pacing back and forth. A few minutes later he heard a voice say, "Josh". He turned and saw Jessica coming toward him at a fast-walking pace. She hugged him and said, "I'm so glad you're here."

"How is she?" Josh asked.

"Let's talk while we walk. We have to take the elevator. The doctors think she'll be okay but she's going to need a lot of rehab." Jessica said.

They arrived at the elevator and Jessica pushed the 'up' button. The elevator door opened, and they moved inside. Jessica said, "Listen, Josh, there's more you should know. I tried to tell you yesterday, but you hung up before I could. Em has more injuries than I told you about. Her left leg is broken, and she has a black eye and a few lacerations on her face. Also…she can't move her toes. The doctors think whoever did this to her may have damaged her spine. She may never walk again."

"Sonofabitch", Josh replied. "When will they know for sure?"

"They said it would be a few days. They want to give her some time to recover from the surgery they did on her leg and wiring her mouth closed."

Silence for a moment then Josh said, "Who did this to her?"

The door of the elevator opened, and they walked out. Jessica led him down a long corridor toward Emily's room. She said, "I don't know. She either won't say or can't say. She uses a pen and pad to communicate."

"What did the cops say?"

"They don't have any suspects right now. The only evidence they have is Emily and she isn't talking to them."

"How did this happen? Where was she?" Josh asked emphatically

"She had just closed the bar, and we think she was getting in her car when she was attacked. I'm the one who found her.

When she didn't come home by 3:00, I got worried and walked to the bar to see if she was still there. We only live a couple of blocks away. I found her lying on the concrete behind the bar where she always parks. She was about ten feet away from her car. I have my own keys to the bar, so I ran in and called 911."

"Then you followed the ambulance in her car?"

"That's right. Wait…how did you know?"

"I saw her Camaro in the parking lot when I drove in last night."

They arrived at Emily's room and Jessica said, "Before we go in, you should prepare yourself. She doesn't look good."

"Is she awake?"

"She should be. She was when I told her you were here. She's anxious to see you."

Jessica opened the door to the room and Josh took a deep breath. He wanted to prepare himself for the worst. When he entered, he noticed the windowsill had several flower bouquets and 'get well soon' greeting cards placed on it. Emily had an IV in her arm and a neck brace around her neck. Emily couldn't turn her head, so Josh had to walk closer to his sister. He said, "Hey, sis."

Emily tried to smile, and a tear rolled down the side of her face. The head of her bed had been raised up and she had a rolling table in front of her. There was a notepad with a pen and pencil on the table and a bottle of water with a straw in it. Josh went to her and placed his hand on her head. "I'm here, Em"

Emily strained to swallow and tried desperately to speak. Josh told her "Don't try to talk."

She grabbed the notepad and pen and began to write. Josh stopped her and said, "Hang on a sec." He gently took the pad from her hand tore a blank sheet from it and placed the sheet directly on the table. He said, "Don't write on paper still in the notepad. Trust me."

She wrote: 'Glad you're here'

Josh read it and said, "Anything for my big Sis."

Josh turned to Jessica and said, "Could you give us a few minutes?"

Jessica said, "Sure. I'll go downstairs and get a cup of coffee." And she walked out.

Josh asked Emily, "Do you know who did this to you?"

He looked at Emily's right thumb that was pointed up. He said, "Good idea. Thumbs up for 'yes' and thumbs down for 'no'."

He said, "Who was it?"

Emily hesitated then wrote, 'Derek Johnson'

"Have you told the cops?"

Thumb down

"Why not.? Did this Derek threaten you?"

Thumbs up. She wrote, 'said he would cut my throat.'

Josh grabbed the sheet she had written on, folded it, and stuffed it into his jeans pocket. Then he tore another sheet from the notepad and placed it in front of her.

"Okay," Josh said. "When do you expect to see the doctor?"

She wrote, 'soon'.

Josh said, "I would like to speak to him."

Thumbs up.

"Has your adoptive mom been up to see you?"

Thumbs up

"Do you expect her soon?"

Thumbs down then she wrote, 'afternoon'.

"Good", Josh said, "The fewer people that know I'm here, the better."

Emily wrote '?'

"I'm going to fix this. Jessica says the cops have no evidence and you gave me this Derek guy's name. I'm going to need to borrow Jessica for a while. Is that Okay?"

Thumbs up

"I also think she should leave town for a couple of days while I take care of things."

Thumbs up

"How much do you trust her?" Josh asked.

Emily pointed at her heart and made a circle with her finger.

"All of your heart. Got it."

Moments later, a handsome man in his upper 20s entered the room. He was wearing scrubs and a lab coat. The man said to Emily, "Good morning, Sunshine. How are you feeling?'

Emily gave him a thumbs-up and pointed at Josh.

The man came to Josh with an outstretched hand and said, "I'm Doctor Hinson."

Josh shook his hand and said, "Joshua Bailey, Emily's brother."

"Oh," The doctor said, "Pleasure to meet you."

Josh said, "Give it to me straight, Doc. What's the prognosis?"

The Doctor said, "Well, as you can see, she has a broken leg, a black eye and we had to wire her jaw closed. We plan to remove the neck brace this afternoon."

"How long will it be before she can talk again?" Josh asked.

"We expect only a week or two."

"What else?"

"We're concerned that she doesn't have any feeling in her toes. We need her to rest, and we'll see. It could clear up on its own." The Doctor turned his attention to his patient, smiled, and said, "We're going to get you through this, Em. It's going to take a lot of work, but I believe you'll be fine in a couple of months. How's the pain?"

Thumbs down and she pointed to her broken leg.

"Okay," He said, "Continue with the morphine drip. When the pain gets to be too much, tap the button."

Thumbs up.

"I'll be in to check on you this afternoon." The Doctor said. He turned to Josh and said, "Pleasure to meet you." He continued, "We'll take good care of your sister" and he exited the room.

Josh said, "He seems nice. Husband material maybe?"

Emily rolled her eyes and tried a slight smile.

Josh was staring out the 3rd-floor window. Emily tapped the table with her pen to get Josh's attention. Josh looked at her as she wrote. 'Tired. Need sleep'

Josh nodded and said "Get some rest. I'll try to get back up here later today."

He bent down and stroked her hair and whispered in her ear. "Don't worry about a thing. Love you." Then he kissed her forehead.

He rose up and Emily pointed to her heart then to Josh.

Josh grabbed the paper she wrote on folded it like the last one and put it in his pocket. She tore off another sheet and wrote another question mark. Josh picked up the notepad and drew a circle on it. Then he found a pencil, moved the sheet he wrote on, and brushed the pencil sideways on the next sheet. An indentation appeared on the sheet showing the circle he had just written. He showed it to her, and she gave him a thumbs up. He said, "An old detective's trick."

He gave her a knowing nod of his head and walked out the door. He saw Jessica coming his way from the elevator. As she approached him, he said, "I need your help."

Josh and Jessica walked out of the main entrance and toward Josh's pickup. He said, "We need to go for a ride, and I need information. Emily knows you're with me. She's sleeping."

"What do you want to know?" She asked.

"First," Josh said, "I need you to trust me and do exactly what I say. It's for your and Emily's protection. Can you do that?"

Jessica nodded.

Josh said, "I need a verbal answer. Nothing you do for the rest of your life will be as important as the help you provide for me today. I'm putting a lot of trust in you because Emily says I can. I need you to do the same thing."

"Yes," she said.

They climbed into the truck, but Josh hadn't started the

engine yet. He said, "What can you tell me about Derek Johnson?"

"I fucking knew it," Jessica exclaimed. "Is he the one who did this to her?"

"What do you know about him?" was Josh's response.

"What do you want to know?" she asked.

"Everything," Josh said. "What does he look like? What does he drive? Where does he work? Does he have family here? Most importantly, where does he live? Everything."

Jessica told him everything she knew about him, which was a lot. She said that she and Emily had known him for years. He was always trying to get her to go out with him. Emily always turned him down. She said he owns a used car dealership in town. That he has a house out in the country. She also believed, as did most people, that he was a coke dealer.

Josh started the truck and said, "Show me where his work is."

They pulled out of the parking lot and Jessica gave him directions. After a few turns, Jessica said, "That's his dealership down there on the right."

They drove about a half block and Josh slowed just a little as they passed the lot. He said, "Do you see his car there?"

Jessica said, "No."

"What does he normally drive?"

She said, "A black Corvette."

They drove on further, and Josh said, "Show me where he lives."

Jessica gave him directions and a few moments later they were almost in the country away from the busy city streets.

She said, "Keep going down this road for about five miles and I'll let you know where to turn."

Josh asked, "What else can you tell me about him?"

Jessica thought for a moment then said, "Well, about two years ago, he was a 'person of interest' in a murder case. Her name was Caitlin Monroe. She was fifteen and was found beaten, raped, and stabbed to death. Her body was found not far from his house."

"Jesus," Josh said, "Why wasn't he charged?"

Jessica said, "If I remember right, the word on the street was that they couldn't find the murder weapon and he had an alibi."

"Let me guess. He was hanging out with three of his friends at a party the night she was murdered, and the three friends alibied him."

"Something like that," Jessica said, "The prosecutor said they didn't have enough evidence to charge him. The case was never solved."

Josh shook his head and mumbled, "Fucking courts."

They turned down a gravel road surrounded by corn fields. The stalks were nearly seven feet tall. He said, "When does corn harvest start here?"

Jessica said that most farmers will begin cutting this week. Then she said, "Another mile down on the left. It's a white house with an attached garage."

They approached the house and Josh slowed just a bit but didn't stop. He scanned the area and asked Jessica where the road led to. She told him that at the next intersection, half a mile down, a right turn would take them back to town and a left turn would take them to the Missouri River. She wasn't sure how far the road they were on went or where it ended. Josh continued to drive and turned right at the next corner heading back to town. It was another gravel road that lasted for a couple of miles until the road became asphalt.

Josh said, "You need to get out of town for a couple of days. Do you have friends in Kansas City?"

"I have several friends there," Jessica replied.

"Good", Josh said, "Let's go to your apartment so you can get a few things then I'll take you back to the hospital so you can get Emily's car. Then I want you to go directly to your friends' home in Kansas City."

"Why?" Jessica asked.

"It's for your own safety." He continued. "When you get there, you need to be seen. Go to bars, restaurants, or the mall. Anywhere public. Do you have a credit card?"

Jessica nodded 'yes'.

"Excellent. Use it as much as you can over the next forty-eight hours. You don't have to buy a lot of things. But use it at the places I mentioned and get receipts. Stay in public as much as you can and don't go anywhere alone once you get there. Tell your friends that the cops here think it's best for you to get out of town for a couple of days. Do NOT tell them about me."

"I don't understand all this," she said.

"If this Derek Johnson knows that you and Emily are close, and I assume he does," Josh stated. "Getting out of town and going to KC will be the safest thing for you to do."

"I really don't like this, but I'll do it," Jessica said.

"I promise I'll explain it to you in a few days. I told you that I need you to trust me. It's for your own safety."

They drove back into town and Jessica gave him directions to her and Emily's apartment. Suddenly Jessica said, "Sonofabitch, there he is."

"Where?" Josh asked.

"Down there. On the opposite side of the street." She said, "Shit, that's his 'Vette parked right in front of our building."

Josh said, "Turn away and look out the window on your side. Don't turn back until I tell you."

They passed by where the Corvette was parked, and Josh glanced over to see if anyone was in it. There was. When they got further down the street, Josh said. "You can look forward now. We're clear."

"Was he in his car?" Jessica asked.

"There was someone in it. I don't know if it was Johnson or not. The guy I saw had short, curly, blonde, almost white hair"

"That's him. What the fuck is he doing sitting in front of our apartment?"

"He's waiting for you."

"Why?" Jessica asked.

"Because he wants to find out if Emily told you what he did to her. That's why. You saw what he did to her. You don't think he'd hesitate to do the same to you?"

They turned around in a parking lot and came back the other way. This time the Corvette would be on the same side of the street that they were driving on. "Duck down," Josh told her. "We can't let him see you in my truck. He won't be able to see you. We're too tall and he doesn't know my pickup."

Jessica did as she was told. As they drove past the Vette,

Josh made a mental note of the license plate. They continued to the hospital. Josh was making sure that Derek Johnson wasn't following them. As they pulled into the hospital parking lot, Josh asked, "It's Friday. Where will he most likely be tonight?"

"Normally he would be at our bar but since it's closed, he'll most likely be at Twisters."

Josh said, "Sounds like a country bar."

Jessica nodded and said, "A big one."

"Okay, I'll look up the address in the phone book. I'll find it."

They pulled up in front of Emily's Camaro and Josh stopped the truck. He said, "Do not go to your apartment. Get in Emily's car and head straight to Kansas City. Be wary of any cars that may be following you. Take I29 down and don't get pulled over."

"I won't. I'll go directly to my friend's house, and I'll do what you said."

"Good," Josh said, "Stay in public as much as you can until late, and don't leave yourself alone. Make sure you always have someone with you. Do not stay in a hotel either. You must have people you trust with you the whole time you're there."

"I will," she said.

"Come back in two days. I'll call the hospital to check on Emily and talk to you then. Two days" He reiterated.

Josh found the office for the St. Joseph News-Press. He went inside and spoke to the receptionist. He said, "My name is John Bishop and I'm a student at UMKC in Kansas City. I'm doing research for a paper I'm writing and I'm wondering if you could help me."

The very nice receptionist said, "I'll certainly try. What are you looking for?"

Josh said, "A couple of years ago, there was a young lady by the name of Caitlin Monroe who had been murdered. I was wondering if you could tell me the date it happened and show me any articles written about the case."

The lady said, "That was such a horrible day. I remember it well. It was in March of 1987"

"I wonder if you could direct me to your archives," Josh said.

"I'd be happy to." She said.

She led him down a corridor and into a room that was filled with old newspapers. She scanned the aisles and found 1987, then March. She pulled the large wood bar that was resting on hooks and carried the large bundle of papers to a table nearby. As she sat it down, she said. "I'm sure you'll find the articles in this bunch."

Josh said, "Thank you so much for your assistance."

She told him he was welcome and disappeared back to her desk.

Josh began scouring the papers, focusing on the front pages and scanning the headlines. It wasn't long before a headline caught his eye. It said, 'LOCAL TEENAGER BEATEN, RAPED AND STABBED. Josh started reading the article. It was just like Jessica said. A local teenage girl, 15, was found dead in a secluded area just north of St. Joseph, according to a report issued by the sheriff's office. The article went on to say that the girl's name was Caitlin Monroe of St. Joseph. Later in the story, it stated that the Sheriff's office had a 'person of interest' but wouldn't say who that person was. It was too early in the investigation. It wasn't much help to Josh, so he checked the next day's paper and found a headline that said, 'MURDER SUSPECT CLEARED'. The article stated that Derek Johnson had been questioned in the disappearance of Caitlin and that his alibi was checked and confirmed. Sheriff Ralph Hendricks was quoted, "We currently have no other suspects, and the murder weapon has not been found." When asked about Caitlin, her father Richard Monroe said, "We want whoever did this to pay for what they've done. Caitlin was a sweet girl and did not deserve what happened to her." He asked if anyone had any information to please contact the Buchanan County Sheriff's office.

Josh placed the bunch of papers back on the hooks. Strolled back to the front of the office and thanked the nice lady for her help. "I hope it was helpful. Good luck with your paper.", she said.

Josh found a telephone directory for St. Joseph and looked up Richard Monroe. He discovered an R. Monroe and no other Monroe's were listed in the book. The address for R. Monroe was listed as 1305 S. Oak Street. Across the street from the St. Joseph News-Press was the St. Joseph Chamber of Commerce. He walked across the street and entered the building where he found a large rack of pamphlets of things to see and do near St. Joesph. What he was looking for was a city map. He found one.

He got back in the truck and opened the map. There were landmarks prominently marked. The Chamber of Commerce, the hospital where Emily was, and where each church was located. He found the numbered streets and followed them with his finger until he found Oak Street. The city blocks were all in squares, which made it easier. He memorized the directions and started driving. He was traveling down 8th street and found Oak. He turned left and as he drove, paid attention to the green street signs indicating each cross street as well as the numbers on the homes. He learned that 1305 Oak would be on the left side and would most likely be the third house from the corner. He reached 15th Street and slowed, checking the house numbers that were painted on the curb in front of each house. He counted them off. 1301, 1303, and 1305. He pulled another 20 feet down and parked the truck along the curb. He got out, crossed the street, and walked back toward 1305 Oak Street.

The house was run down from neglect. It used to be white but needed paint or siding badly, the grass was turning brown from the fall temperatures and as he approached the small steps leading to the front door, he noticed the handrails on either side of the stairs were crooked and looked very unstable. The porch was narrow and had two white wicker chairs and a small table between them. He carefully climbed the steps and came to a screen door that was barely hanging on by its hinges. He didn't see a doorbell, so he knocked on the screen door which rattled against the door jamb. Suddenly and quickly the inner door opened and a scruffy-looking man with a five-day growth of beard said, "Whatever you're selling, we ain't buying"

Josh said, "Sir, I'm not selling anything. I wonder if I could ask you some questions."

The man said, "No" and slammed the door shut.

Josh said in a loud voice. "What if I told you I can get justice for your daughter?"

The door opened slowly, and the man had a questioning look on his face. He said, "And just how do plan on doing that?"

Josh said, "Sir, my name is John Bishop and I'm here to help. Are you Richard Monroe, father of Caitlin Monroe?"

The man nodded and Josh said, "If I could just ask you a few questions, I promise it won't take long."

Richard Monroe opened the screen door and told Josh to have a seat in one of the wicker chairs on the porch.

"What do you want to know?" He asked Josh.

Josh said, "First I want to offer my condolences on your loss. Allow me to explain what I do. I am an advocate for victims of families who have lost loved ones and who the courts and law enforcement have failed. When I was a kid, my mother was murdered by a man who should have been locked up, but the courts failed to do their job. I help people rectify that."

Richard said, "I'm listening."

Josh said, "I'm already aware of your daughter's case but what I want to find out from you is how you and your family were treated by law enforcement and the courts."

"Bunch of assholes," Richard said. "We told the Sheriff who we were convinced killed our daughter. This guy, his name is Derek Johnson. He came from a wealthy family here in town. Both of his parents died and left him some money. Now he owns a used car dealership here in town, but I think it's just a front for a drug business." He continued, "This piece of shit Johnson had been stalking our Caitlin for months. He was three years older than her. After we told the investigators about him, they questioned him and then released him."

"Why?" Josh asked.

"They said he had an alibi. He told them he was at a party with some friends the night Caitlin was killed. The Sheriff said that they checked and three of his friends 'verified' it."

Josh nodded his head, "I've heard of this happening before. Did the Sheriff at least get a search warrant for Johnson's house?"

"That's the real kick in the ass. He asked the judge for it, but the judge refused. Judge Harold Wolfson, fucking ingrate, he told them that he couldn't issue a search warrant based only on what we told them and because Johnson had an alibi, there wasn't enough evidence to justify a search warrant."

Josh thought for a moment then he said, "Sir, I have every intention of getting justice for your daughter. I believe every word you've said, and you certainly have no reason to lie to me."

Richard sat silently looking out at the street. Then he said, "Why are you doing this?"

Josh said, "Because it's past time for the courts, law enforcement, and the law itself to be held accountable for their blatant stupidity and not giving a rat ass about the victims and their families."

"So, what can a young kid like you do about it?" Richard asked.

Josh said, "I'm afraid I can't tell you that. The less you

know the better. In fact, it's best that no one knows that I spoke to you. No one knows I'm here and no one ever will if you don't tell anyone. I work alone and I am very secretive."

Richard said, "You'll understand that I'm skeptical that you can do anything."

"I do," Josh said. "I'd be skeptical too."

Josh thanked him for his time for answering his questions and for his honesty. He walked to his pick-up, got in, and began formulating his plan.

It was nearing lunchtime, and Josh found a Sonic drive-in. He pulled into a spot, ordered his lunch, and awaited the arrival of his food. When it arrived, he thanked the curb hop, paid her with cash, and gave her a substantial tip.

Josh drove back toward Derek Johnson's home in the country. This time, instead of turning right at the next intersection, he turned left toward the Missouri River. He noticed a 'Dead End' sign and continued down the gravel road. A mile later he came across a barricade at the end of the road. He placed the truck in 'park', got out, and walked toward the river. He noticed what used to be an old boat ramp leading into the river. What little concrete was left of the ramp was now filled with cracks. He looked across the river and noticed no homes or buildings on the other side. Just a tree line. Then he looked upriver and saw a railroad trestle that crossed the river a quarter mile away. On his side of the river was another tree line. The trees stretched from the riverbank to about fifteen feet before meeting the corn fields. He wondered if Caitlin Monroe's body had been found amongst the trees. He nodded his head and said to himself. "This will do nicely".

Josh checked his watch. It was almost 6:00 p.m. A time when most people would be home eating dinner. He decided that would be the best time to visit Emily. He thought that her adoptive mother would be home. It wasn't as if he didn't want to meet her. Just not today. On his way to the hospital, he passed by the used car dealership to see if the black Corvette was there. It wasn't. Then he drove past Emily and Jessica's apartment. The Vette was gone.

Before going to Emily's room, Josh called Lisa from a payphone in the hospital lobby as promised. He said he was on his way to see Emily again.

Josh knocked lightly on Emily's hospital room door and slowly entered. Emily was awake and sitting up. Her neck brace had been removed so she could turn her head better. When she saw him, she smiled ever so slightly.

Josh walked over to her and bent down to kiss her forehead. He said, "How ya feeling, Sis?"

She wiggled her hand 'so-so'.

She grabbed her notepad removed a sheet from it and placed it flat on the table. She wrote, 'Where you have been?'

Josh said he spent the morning with Jessica getting information.

She wrote, 'I know'. She paused then wrote, 'Called me from KC'

"Good," Josh said.

'My mom answered the phone'

'Put the phone to my ear'

'Listened to one of our friends there too'

Josh said, "I'm glad she got there safe."

Emily wrote '?'

"It was for her safety." Josh said, "Derek Johnson was parked in front of your apartment...waiting."

Emily wrote, 'shit'.

"How's your...mom?"

Thumbs up.

Emily wrote, 'You, ok?'

Josh nodded.

She wrote, 'Glad you're here'

Josh smiled and said, "Me too, Sis." Then he said, "Aunt Lo and Lisa send their best. They're worried about you."

Emily tapped her heart with her hand.

Josh said, "They love you too."

Josh picked up the paper she had been writing on and put it in his pocket with the others from that morning. He said, "I have something I have to do tonight then I'm heading home in the morning. I probably won't be able to come back for a while."

Emily drew a circle on another piece of paper and made a frowning face on it.

"It'll be okay," Josh promised. "Everything will be made right soon."

Emily wrote in all capital letters, 'PLEASE BE CAREFUL.'

"I will," Josh said.

A tear began streaming down Emily's face. Josh grabbed her hand with one hand stroked her hair with his other and bent down to whisper in his sister's ear, "You'll get your justice tonight, I promise."

Emily squeezed Josh's hand tightly.

He whispered, "He'll get what's coming to him."

She tapped her heart with her free hand and touched Josh's chest with it. Josh bent down again and kissed her forehead.

He said, "Have Jessica call me when she gets back in a couple of days, please. Tell her to use a pay phone. Not the phone in here."

Emily made an 'X' over her heart with her finger.

Josh picked up the last notepaper she wrote on and put it in his pocket.

* * *

Twister's dance hall sat alone east of St. Joe. Jessica had been right, it was big. Neon green and red lights brightened the gravel parking lot in front of the building. There was an almost comical painting of a tornado next to the 'Twister's' neon sign. Josh parked his black pickup facing the bar in a vacant lot across the road, shut off the headlights, and turned off the engine. He watched as several cars rolled into the dirty, dusty lot. He checked his watch, it was 8:00. A few moments later he saw the black Corvette enter the lot and park. Derek Johnson got out of the Corvette and started toward the door. Josh noticed the bright almost white curly hair that he had seen earlier in the day with Jessica. Derek Johnson was tall, at least 6'3", lanky. He was dressed in jeans and a snap button shirt. Josh was surprised that he wasn't wearing a Stetson. He watched as Johnson strode to the door of the club. He walked as if he was the king of the world. The word 'cocky' came to Josh's mind.

He waited and watched patiently for four hours then decided it was time to put his plan to work. He drove out of the lot and made his way to his secret hiding place at the end of the dead-end road. The moon was full, and the sky was still clear. As he came within ¼ mile of Johnson's house he slowed down considerably so the pickup wouldn't create as much dust and attract any attention and turned off his headlights, allowing the moon glow to guide him the rest of the way. As he reached the corner and turned, he was careful not to use his brakes to keep the brake lights from illuminating. When he got to the barricade, he turned the truck around so it would be facing the way he needed to depart.

He got out opened the toolbox and grabbed his large canvas duffle bag. He opened the bag took out what he needed and placed it on the tailgate. He stripped down to his underwear and put on a pair of black Levi's jeans, a black, long-sleeved t-shirt a pair of black socks, and an all-black baseball cap which he wore backwards, and put on his pull-up black boots. Then he picked up a small makeup container that he had used before on Halloween. He spread the black makeup over his face. Not completely covered but enough to distort his face if anyone saw him from a distance. He put the clothes he had just removed into the canvas bag along with the makeup container.

He went back to the toolbox and picked up his leather gloves and put them on. He would be wearing them for the rest of the night. Then he reached into the box and pulled out Woody's Springfield gun case, unzipped it, and removed the rifle. Using an old, greasy rag and with his gloved hands, wiped the gun completely. Then he took one 30.06 bullets from his small ammo box. There were only three rounds left in it. He placed the bullet into the bolt and chambered the round. He set the rifle aside and picked up everything that was loose placed it all in the canvas bag, zipped it closed, and put it back into the toolbox. He closed the tailgate, slung the rifle over his shoulder, and began walking.

The moonlight was very helpful. Josh couldn't have picked a better night to complete his mission. He walked into the corn field and passed two rows of very tall corn stalks. He followed the row until he arrived at the dirt road intersection. He looked left and right making sure there were no vehicles coming down the road. When he felt it was clear, he jogged quickly across the road into the cornfield that lay across the road from Johnson's house. He turned right and stayed between the third and fourth rows of corn. When he got about 50 feet from his destination, he got down on the ground and crawled the rest of the way to his chosen spot.

Josh lay prone and took the rifle from across his back. Laying between stalks of corn, he peered through the scope and had an excellent view of Johnson's house and garage. He figured that he was no more than 75 yards from the garage door. Much closer than he needed to be. He checked his watch. It was almost 1:30. Patience.

As he waited, Josh had visions of Emily lying in her hospital bed. Hurting, broken, and scared. He also imagined Caitlin Monroe being beaten, raped and stabbed. Left to die alone. He had seen enough injustice and would do everything in his ability to end as much of it as he could.

At around 2:15 he saw the glow of headlights coming from his left. As the vehicle approached it slowed down. The black Corvette pulled into the driveway and up to the garage. The automatic garage door began to rise and the motion sensor light above the garage lit up. Josh peered through the scope of the Springfield and watched as Derek Johnson slowly pulled the Vette into the garage. He got out of the Vette with a small gym bag in his hand. Josh aimed the crosshairs at Derek's head, took a breath, exhaled, and squeezed the trigger.

The bullet entered the right side of Derek Johnson's head and exited out the other side. Blood spewed and sprayed the opposite wall of the garage. Derek collapsed to the concrete floor still holding the gym bag in his right hand.

Josh hesitated a moment to see if there was any

movement. The motion sensor lights went dark. Josh slung the rifle across his back. Time to go.

Josh, you only get one shot at life, and it only takes one shot to end a life.

* * *

Josh made his way back to the pickup the same way he came. Crawling the first 50 feet then walking briskly the rest of the way. He checked the corner carefully again and then darted across the road.

When he arrived at the pickup, he reached into the cab and pulled out the paper bag that his Sonic food had been in then he opened the toolbox, grabbed the large canvas bag, and carried it to the back of the pickup. He removed the black clothing and boots placed all of them into the large bag and put on the clothes he had worn earlier. He found two rocks near the shore of the river, at least ten pounds each, and placed them in the bag with the clothing. He dug the notes that Emily had written out of his pocket and put them into the Sonic bag then wiped his face with several moist towelettes to remove the black makeup placing each one in the Sonic bag and putting the Sonic bag into the larger canvas bag. He cut a small slit into the top and bottom of the canvas bag to allow water to get in and air to escape quickly.

Then he picked up the rifle and holding it sideways worked the bolt. The lone shell case fell with a 'clink' onto the truck bed. He picked it up and put it in his old school backpack. He then dismantled the rifle, making sure to remove all the metal parts. He had done this many times and could most likely do it blindfolded. He removed the trigger, bolt, and the barrel. He set the barrel aside placed the remaining parts into his backpack and put the gun stock into the large bag. Then he removed his gloves and put them into the canvas bag with the other items.

He slung the backpack over his shoulders, picked up the canvas bag with one hand and the gun barrel with his other, and began walking toward the railroad trestle. When he arrived at the railroad tracks, he checked left and right. Looking and listening for a possible train to approach. He stepped carefully onto the railroad ties and walked across the trestle making sure he stepped on the ties. When he got about 30 feet from land, he tossed the canvas bag out into the water. He heard it splash and was just able to see the bag sink into the Missouri River. Then he threw the rifle barrel as far as he could in the opposite direction of the bag. He reached into his backpack and one at a time threw the metal parts and shell casing into the river making sure they went in different directions. He put the backpack over his shoulders and walked back toward the pickup. Just as he stepped onto solid ground, he heard a train whistle off in the distance.

* * *

Josh looked in the review mirror and checked his face for any makeup he may have missed. Clean.

He started the pickup and drove down the road using the bright moonlight to guide him. He crossed the intersection and resisting the urge to go past Johnson's house continued straight toward town. As he crossed the intersection, he looked to his right toward the house and saw no flashing lights. He checked his watch. It was 4:00 a.m.

When he reached the point where the gravel turned to asphalt, he turned on his headlights. He drove through town making sure not to attract attention by speeding and found 129. He turned right onto the ramp to 29 South and entered the interstate.

Several miles south of St. Joseph sat the Farris Truck Stop. Josh pulled in and found a place to park behind the building among a few other vehicles. He turned off the engine, laid his head on the steering wheel, and fell asleep.

When he woke up it was 7:00 a.m. He walked into the truck stop, used the restroom, and used a pay phone to call Lisa. She answered and he told her he was on his way and would be home around noon.

As he drove, he went over everything in his head. Fingerprints, none. He had worn his gloves, and they were now destroyed. Boot prints, maybe a few might be discovered but the boots were also destroyed. No way to match them. He had no gunshot residue on his hands or arms from wearing his gloves and the long-sleeved T-shirt. His weapon was dismantled and would not be found for 100 years or more. The only purchase he made was at Sonic and he used cash. No one saw him on the gravel road. The only evidence he left behind was the slug that went through Derek Johnson's head. It couldn't be traced back to any weapon that had been used in a crime. Investigators would spend hours looking for evidence and they would only find the bullet. When he got back to Anthony, he would put new tires on the truck as an added precaution.

* * *

On Monday the phone rang at Lo's house. Josh answered and it was Jessica. Josh asked how Emily was doing. Jessica said she seemed to be doing better. Her black eye was beginning to heal. But the best part was that she was able to move her toes slightly.

"That's terrific news," Josh said.

Jessica said, "I understand now why you wanted me to go to Kansas City and use my credit card."

"Are you calling from a pay phone?" He asked.

Jessica replied, "Yes".

Josh said, "Don't say any names. All I can tell you is that in addition to keeping you safe, you needed to establish an alibi in case you were questioned."

She said, "I understand that now."

Josh said, "Give my love to Emily and tell her to call me as soon as she's able to speak."

Jessica assured him that she would.

* * *

On that Friday, seven days after he left St, Joseph, Josh received a package. The postmark was from St. Joe and the return address said E. Baker. Inside were two things. A VHS tape and a newspaper article from the St. Joseph News-Press.

Josh read the newspaper article first, the headline read: SUSPECTED DRUG DEALER SHOT, KILLED. The article said that a man, Derek Johnson had been found dead inside his garage on Monday morning. He was discovered by a postal employee who was delivering mail at Johnson's rural home. Sheriff Quinton Manzarek said that the victim was found in his opened garage with an apparent gunshot wound to the head. A preliminary investigation by the Medical Examiner stated that the crime occurred sometime late Friday night or early Saturday morning. Johnson was found with a gym bag still in his hand which contained two pounds of white powder suspected to be cocaine. Testing of the substance would be forthcoming. The Sheriff went on to say that a routine search of the victim's home uncovered a large amount of what they believed was also cocaine. They also found numerous firearms.

"We also discovered a large knife hidden under a floorboard. It appears to have some blood on it. We're sending it to be DNA tested." He continued. "At the risk of making assumptions, we believe the knife had been used in the death of Caitlin Monroe two years ago when Mr. Johnson was a suspect in her case, but we'll have to wait for DNA testing to be completed to be certain."

"We also believe the shooting was the act of a disgruntled drug buyer. So far, the only evidence we have recovered was the bullet that had penetrated the inner wall of the garage." The sheriff noted.

The article went on about Johnson's past, his parents and upbringing, and the car dealership.

Josh folded the article and put it back in the package. Then with the tape in his hand, he went to his bedroom, and turned on his television and VCR. He put the tape in the player and pushed play.

It was a news story from some TV station in St. Joseph. The on-scene reporter was talking about the shooting, and it had the Sheriff stating the same things as the newspaper article. The reporter said, "We spoke to Richard Monroe, father of murder victim, Caitlin Monroe earlier in the day. Here's what he had to say."

The video switched to Richard Monroe who was being interviewed. At the bottom of the screen was the phrase: Richard Monroe father of Caitlin Monroe. The interviewer asked, "What are you feeling today with the possibility that your daughter's killer has been shot?"

Richard told the interviewer, "We told them two years ago he was the one who killed our daughter, but no one believed us. They'll believe us now when the DNA results come back."

Richard looked directly into the camera and said, "Whoever did this, thank you. We finally get some closure and will sleep better knowing this horrible human being can no longer hurt anyone."

Josh removed the tape from the VCR and placed it back in the package with the newspaper article. Then he took the package out to his pickup and put it in the glove box. He would burn all of it tonight.

CHAPTER 16

Two weeks later, the phone rang at Lo's house and Josh answered. He immediately recognized his sister's voice. "Hey, little brother." She said.

"Hey, Sis!" Josh exclaimed. "It's so good to hear your voice again. "

"It's good to be able to use it again." Emily quipped.

"Are you out of the hospital yet?"

Emily said she had been out for a couple of days and that they unwired her jaw just an hour ago.

"So, then you're able to walk too? Your spine injury is, ok?"

"With crutches. My leg is still in a cast, but my doctor says I should be able to get rid of them in a few weeks."

Josh asked, "Is that the same doctor that I think you should marry?"

Emily giggled and said, "Stop."

"Think about it. You would have premium health care and wouldn't have to pay for it."

"Quit," she said.

Josh asked about Jessica. She was doing good, Emily told him, and the Steakhouse was doing well also. She said that she's able to go in and take care of a few things every day.

Then Emily said, "Little brother, I want to thank you...for everything. It's entirely possible that you saved my life"

"No need to thank me, Sis. There's nothing I wouldn't do for you."

* * *

It was the middle of November. Farm work was done so Josh helped Aunt Lo fix things up at the house. He managed to keep himself occupied. He read a lot during the cold winter months. He was able to see Lisa every day when she got off work from the store. Sometimes, they would have dinner at her house but mostly they ate with Aunt Lo. Loanne loved having them to cook for and they both wanted her to have someone around as much as possible. They knew the holidays would be especially hard on her this year. It would be her first Thanksgiving and Christmas without Woody, so they made sure to include her in everything.

A few days before Thanksgiving, Josh received another newspaper article from Emily. It was a brief story, and it said essentially that the Sheriff's office announced that the blood discovered on the knife found at Derek Johnson's home had been used the murder of Caitlin Monroe. DNA testing had confirmed that fact. Also, the white substance found there was, in fact, cocaine. On a side note: Judge Harold Wolfson, who had denied the Sheriff a search warrant in the case of

Caitlin Monroe's death, retired suddenly and left town. It was believed that he ran off to Florida and went into hiding.

Thanksgiving this year would be at Dan and Nancy's home. This year, Nancy did the turkey and Lo made pumpkin pie...from scratch. "Is there any other way?" Lo would ask.

Throughout the fall and winter, Josh and Lisa and Aunt Lo would attend basketball games at Chaparral to watch Lisa's sister, Lori play. She was quite the athlete, and the Road Runners were having a winning season. When Christmas arrived, both families celebrated at the Fisher home. Gifts were exchanged and another perfect meal was eaten and enjoyed by everyone. They left one open chair at the table in honor of Woody. There was no mention of it, but everyone knew.

On New Year's Eve, Josh and Lisa stayed home with Aunt Lo and watched movies with her until she went to bed. When people do something on one holiday it's just a thing but when you do it twice or more, it becomes a tradition. That was the way Josh and Lisa brought in the New Year. Making love and as Lisa would say, "ringing in the new year the right way."

One cold evening in mid-January, 1990, Lisa had locked up the store. She got into her car and started the engine. Just as she was placing the transmission into 'drive' a figure popped up in the backseat. Lisa was startled and shouted, "Shit"

The man in the back put what felt like a gun into her side and said, "Drive."

"Where?" Lisa asked.

"Just do what I tell you and you won't get hurt." The man said.

He had her make a few turns through town, looking behind them to be sure no one was following. They pulled into an alley and the man told Lisa to turn off the engine and give him the keys. Then the man reached around Lisa's neck and yanked her necklace that Josh had given her from around her neck. Then he told her to get out and not move.

Lisa did as she was told then the unknown man put a blindfold over her eyes and told her to start walking.

"Who are you?" Lisa asked. "What do you want."

The man said, "Just shut up and do what I tell you."

They walked for about 100 feet and the man told her to stop. Then he grabbed her arm and guided her to a set of steps. He said, "Go up these steps and then into the house."

"I can't see," Lisa said.

The man said, "Use your hands and feel for the handrail."

"Now open the door and go inside."

Lisa felt around for a doorknob, found it and turned it to open the door. The man said, "Go inside. There's another set of stairs going down. Find the handrail and make your way down the stairs. Remember, I'm right behind you with a loaded gun pointed at your head so don't do anything stupid."

Lisa said, "My boyfriend will find you and kill you for this."

The man chuckled and said, "You're half right. He'll find us but he won't kill us. You're the bait."

* * *

Josh answered the phone when it rang. The man's voice on the other end said, "If you want to see your little girlfriend alive again, be at the Glickner place in one hour."

Josh said, "Who is this?"

The voice said, "You'll find out when you get there. If I even think there's anyone following you or any cops around, she dies."

Josh said, "I want to talk to her. Right fucking now."

The voice said, "No. Glickner place. One hour. If you want proof, check your pickup." Then the person hung up.

Josh shouted, "FUCK, FUCK, FUCK" and slammed the phone down.

Lo asked, "What the hell?"

"Lisa's been kidnapped."

Josh ran out to his pickup that was parked in the driveway. He noticed a small brown envelope that had been placed between his wiper blade and the windshield. He carefully picked it up by the edge then took it back into the house and went to the kitchen table. Lo got up from her chair in the front room to see what was going on. Josh opened the envelope being very careful not to mess up any possible fingerprints that might be on it. He squeezed the edges with the opening facing down at the table. The envelope opened and his mom's necklace that he gave to Lisa last Valentine's Day fell out and landed on the table with a 'clink'.

* * *

"Did he say what he wanted?" Lo asked.

Josh was pacing back and forth trying to calm down. "No. All he said was for me to be at the Glickner place in an hour."

"Shit," Lo said. "What are you going to do?"

Josh said, "I'm going to go get her."

Josh made a call, and the last thing Lo heard him say was, "Just give me an hour. Then show up."

"Who was that?" Lo asked.

Josh said, "Officer Wilkenson."

The stories about the old Glickner place had been around for decades. Some people believed the home to be haunted. The story was that old man Glickner had murdered his wife there and hung himself. It was a very old house. When it was built it was the only mansion in town. It had been abandoned for many years. Paint had chipped off the entire house including the four large pillars in front. It was two stories tall and probably had 5 bedrooms. The lot it sat on was secluded. The nearest house was half a block away.

Josh drove to the corner nearest the house and parked the truck. The Glickner place was 100 yards from where he parked. He got out of the truck and walked toward an alley that would lead to the old house. It was dark and very cold. Josh was bundled up in his heavy jacket and his fleece lined gloves. He could see his breath, which was not good since he wanted to be as stealthy as possible. He made his way down the alley slowly and cautiously. As he approached the old house, he saw the one car garage that sat behind it. He ducked down for just a moment to see if he could see any movement. He heard what sounded like a lawn mower coming from the house. The house was dark, and he wasn't sure where he was supposed to go. Just then he heard the 'click' of a pistol hammer. He stood up straight and a man's voice behind him said, "Don't fucking turn around. Put your hands on top of your head and walk to the garage."

Josh said, "Who are you? Where's Lisa?"

The voice said, "You'll find out soon enough. Just keep walking and shut up."

Josh did as he was instructed. When he arrived at the garage the voice said, "Put your hands up against the side."

Josh did so and he felt the man's hand tapping his sides and reach around to tap Josh's chest. Then the man tapped Josh's legs. When he felt Josh had no weapons he stepped back and told Josh to turn around and face him.

Josh turned and the man he saw had a scraggly beard and greasy hair. He was about the same size as Josh. "Do you recognize me?" the man asked.

Josh said, "No. Should I?"

The man said, "You got my mom fired from her job."

Josh squinted his eyes and said, "Sam Blackwell?"

Sam said, "I'm surprised you remembered."

"Where's Lisa? That's the last time I'm going to ask.", Josh said.

"She's in the cellar," Sam said. "Turn around and walk up to the backdoor. Don't try anything stupid, my gun is loaded and there's someone else in the cellar with your girlfriend."

"Who?" Josh asked as he turned to face the house. "Your mom?"

ONE SHOT

The man punched Josh hard in the kidney from behind. Josh let out a grunt and started walking. When they got to the base of the steps that led up to the back door, Josh noticed a small generator next to the house. There was an extension cord running from the generator and snaked down through a blacked-out basement window.

"Go inside and directly down the stairs," Sam said.

As they got to the bottom of the rickety old staircase, Josh glanced around the room. It was barely lit with one lone lightbulb hanging from the ceiling. *That explains the generator.* He looked around the large cellar. It was very cold and damp. The room reeked of black mold and cat urine. The walls were made of rock, some of them jagged and the concrete floor had many cracks in it. In one corner of the cellar, he saw a pile of debris. Some pieces of lumber, old metal pipes and other trash that had been left there for 50 years or more.

Sam said, "See that door down there, go knock on it."

Josh walked a little further into the huge cellar and saw a door that appeared to be attached to a separate room. Josh knocked on the door as he was told. Sam shouted out, "He's here."

Josh heard another man's voice from inside the room say, "Bring that asshole in here."

Sam told Josh to open the door and go in. The room had one light hanging from the ceiling just like the other one. When Josh walked in, he saw Lisa lying on her back on an old spring bed, there was no mattress under her, just springs. Her hands were tied to the old, steel head rail above her head and her legs were tied to the foot end. She had a cut over her eye

229

and duct tape over her mouth. She looked at Josh with both fear and relief in her eyes. To his right, he saw someone sitting in an old, wooden chair facing away from him. The man was seated at a card table that had seen better days. Josh noticed several empty beer bottles on the table. Josh said to Lisa, "Don't worry, Babe. I'm' going to get you out of here." Then Josh said to the guy at the table, "I'm here. Let her go."

The man at the table leaned down toward the table and Josh could hear him taking a big sniff. "Mmmm. No," the guy said. "She's here for the party and she's not going anywhere."

Josh was getting agitated but knew he had to keep his cool.

"Sit down, asshole," the guy said still with his back to Josh. Josh sat in a wood chair that was just like the one the guy was sitting in and removed his gloves, tossing them onto the floor. The man tossed a piece of rope back over his shoulder to Sam and said, "Tie him up with his hands behind his back."

Sam said, "Where should I put my gun?'

"Set it down over on that other table near the bed. He's not going anywhere." Sam did what he was told to do then came back and began tying Josh's hands behind him. The man turned to face Josh and he had a .38 pistol in his hand. Josh got a good look at his face and said, "Cole fucking Jensen. I Might have known."

Josh glanced over at Lisa who had hate in her eyes and was shaking her head. She tried mumbling something and Cole looked at her and said, "Shut the fuck up, bitch."

Josh said, "Let her go. It's me you want."

Cole leaned forward in his chair and said, "Let me tell you a little story, Bailey. A few months ago, I was sitting in a bar in

Wichita having a beer when Sam sat down next to me. We got to talking and one thing led to another. Before we knew it, we both realized we were from the same town. I asked him his name and he told me, then I asked if his mother was ever the principal at the Junior High there. He said, 'yeah.' And I said that I remembered her. I think you can see where I'm going with this."

Josh glared at Cole with fire in his eyes. Cole said, "That's just the look I was going for. Anyway, I told Sam about you giving me that cheap shot on my graduation night."

"I didn't give you a cheap shot. You came at me and missed…twice. Everything that happened to you that night, you had coming. Especially when you hit Lisa, you piece of shit. I could have easily killed you, but I didn't. I wish I had now. If you let her go, you may just survive this night."

Cole got up from his chair, walked over to Josh and hit him hard on his mouth. Josh's head was jarred, and blood began to fill his mouth. Josh spit a large amount of blood onto the floor. Lisa was writhing and trying to get away and screaming under the duct tape.

Cole said, "I don't remember it that way."

"That's because you were drunk and stupid," Josh said.

Cole swung again and connected with Josh's right eye.

"Motherfucker." Josh mumbled.

Cole said, "A couple of months after that night I went to Dodge City Community College on a football scholarship. One night, I was caught driving under the influence. I lost my scholarship and was kicked out of school."

Josh said, "Am I supposed to give a shit?"

Cole punched Josh hard in the stomach knocking the air out of him.

"I lost everything because of you, Motherfucker." Cole said.

"Jesus Christ," Josh said. "You're still not taking responsibility for your own actions. Most people learn from their fuck ups and get smarter as they get older but not you. You're even more stupid than you were back then."

Cole punched Josh again in the mouth.

Sam spoke up, "You told me I could have the first shot at him."

Cole looked at Sam and said, "You're right, I did. Drag this prick out of here and have fun. But don't kill him. I'm going to have some fun of my own with my ex-girlfriend. Take your time. Don't rush. We've got all night."

Josh squirmed and tried to get free of the rope. Sam grabbed the back of the chair Josh was seated in and began dragging him out of the room. When they got to the doorway Josh said to Lisa, "Don't worry, Babe, I'll be right back."

Cole laughed and closed the door behind Sam and Josh.

As Sam dragged him further into the center of the cellar, Josh heard a boom box in the other room playing some kind of loud thrash rock. When Sam got done dragging Josh into the middle of the cellar, he came around to face Josh and punched him in his nose. "That's for my mom, motherfucker." Josh's head went back, and blood began oozing from his nose. Josh spit blood on the concrete again and then. "Whatever happened to your mom?"

Sam glared at him at said, "After you got her fired, we left town. A few months later she killed herself."

Josh said, "Well, that's a shame." He continued to wriggle his hands trying to get free of the binding.

Sam said, "You think I don't know about the name you gave her? I didn't know back then but Cole told me that it was your idea to call my mom 'Witch Hazel'."

Josh spit more blood from his mouth and said, "You have to admit, she did look a lot like her."

Sam backhanded Josh across his face.

Josh needed to keep Sam's attention while he tried to free himself from his binding.

Josh said, "It's funny. You know how some people call someone else a son-of-a-bitch? In your case it's literally true. You really are the son of a bitch."

Sam swung and hit Josh on his mouth. More blood filled his mouth and Josh spit again. Josh said, "Let me ask you something, Sam. Were you ever a boy scout?"

Sam laughed and said, "What?"

Josh spit out more blood and said, "I don't know how I could phrase that question any different." He repeated the question more slowly "Were…you…ever…a…boy…scout?"

Sam said, "No."

Josh said, "I didn't think so because you can't tie a rope worth a fuck." and immediately reached around with his now free right hand and squeezed Sam's esophagus. Sam was unable to shout out. Josh stood with his hand still holding Sam's throat and kneed him hard in the crotch. It all happened so fast; Sam had no time to react. With his hand still on Sam's throat, Josh pushed Sam backwards until the back of Sam's head hit the rock wall of the cellar. Josh slammed Sam's head into the wall three times hard until

Sam's eyes rolled up into his head. Josh released his grip on Sam's throat and Sam fell to the floor. Josh had squeezed Sam's throat so hard that a small amount of blood trickled from where Josh's fingernails had penetrated the skin. There was blood coming from the back of Sam's head as he lay there unconscious.

Josh removed the rest of the rope from his left hand and walked over to the pile of debris. He found a 2-inch diameter metal pipe and picked it up with his right hand. On one end of the pipe there was a metal elbow which was designed to send water or whatever in another direction. The pipe was 3 feet long. Josh slapped his left hand with it and said under his breath, "perfect". He quickly walked over to where Sam was lying still. Josh raised the pipe and swung it down hard like an axe chopping wood onto Sam's knee. Josh mumbled quietly, "That should keep you there for a while, asshole."

Josh made his way back to the closed door of the room Lisa was in. The music inside the room was blaring. He stood with his back against the wall and, using the pipe, scratched at the door. He heard Cole inside shout, "Not yet."

Josh scratched at the door again.

* * *

Lisa was struggling to get free as Cole walked over to her with a large knife that he picked up off the table next to the mirror that had the cocaine on it. He took the knife and pressed it to Lisa's throat, bent down close to her face and said. "Now we're gonna have some fun." With his free hand he grabbed the top of Lisa's buttoned shirt and pulled down on it, popping the buttons off. Lisa writhed and struggled to get free, screaming under the duct tape. Cole placed the knife under her bra and with a jerk cut it. He said, "So, I finally get to see your tits, bitch. You wouldn't put out for me in high school so I'm taking it from you now."

Cole went to the foot of the bed and said, "Now if I untie your feet, are you going to be nice and let me get those jeans of yours off?"

Lisa nodded her head, and Cole used his knife to cut one of the ropes that held Lisa's legs down. As soon as he cut it, Lisa reared her knee up toward her chest and kicked at Cole's face as hard as she could connecting the sole of her foot with Cole's face.

Cole said, "You shouldn't have done that.", and backhanded Lisa across the right side of her face.

There was a scratching noise coming from the door. Cole shouted, "Not yet."

Then another scratch. Cole, irritated with the disruption, put the knife back on the table and picked up his .38 with his left hand. He walked to the door, opened it and peered out saying, "What the fuck?"

Josh immediately swung the pipe directly into Cole's forehead, knocking him backward. When the pipe connected, the gun went off and the bullet ricocheted around the rock walls and entered Josh's belly. Josh yelled, "Fuck". With his adrenaline flowing, he raised the pipe and brought the pipe down hard on Cole's gun filled hand. The gun dropped to the floor. Josh kicked the pistol away. Cole staggered backward and fell onto the cold concrete. Josh came over to him quickly and like a golf swing raised the bar back and brought it across the left side of Jacob's face, and just like he did with Sam, slammed the pipe down onto Cole's knee. Cole shouted, "Motherfucker." Then Josh hit Cole's right forearm shattering the bone. Cole screamed out in pain. With both of Cole's arms broken, Josh was able to place the open end of the pipe directly on Cole's bottom jaw. Part of the pipe opening was in Cole's mouth and the other under his chin. Josh raised his hand up and brought it down onto the elbow end of the pipe. He did it with so much force, he snapped Cole's chin down to his chest. Cole lay there bleeding badly from the head wound and the side of his head. No amount of cocaine would calm the pain he was feeling now. All Cole could do was groan incoherently, but he was still alive.

Josh tossed the pipe, and it landed with a loud clank against the wall. He picked up the knife from the table and quickly moved to Lisa. He said, "I'm going to take that tape off. This might hurt a bit," he grabbed the edge of the tape and with one swift move yanked it from Lisa's face."

Lisa said, "Oh my god, Josh."

Josh cut the rope from Lisa's wrists, and she quickly wrapped her arms around his neck holding him tightly and kissing his neck repeatedly. Josh said, "Are you alright? Can you walk?"

Lisa said with her heart beating fast, "I think so."

Josh said while cutting Lisa's other leg free, "I need to get you out of here." He removed his coat and wrapped it around Lisa's shoulders. Lisa looked down and shouted, "Josh, you're hurt. You're bleeding."

"I'll be alright." Then he walked over to pick up the pipe

that he tossed and brought it to Lisa. He said, "You want to take a shot at him?", and handed her the pipe.

Lisa looked at the pipe then looked at Cole who was lying motionless on the floor. She took the pipe from Josh and went to stand over Cole. Cole was staring up at her with fear in his eyes. Josh said, "Pick a body part but don't kill him."

Lisa asked, "Why not?"

Josh said, "Because that's too good for him. Too easy. He needs to suffer in prison. They both do."

Lisa nodded and like a golfer raised the pipe and swung as hard as she could between Jacobs legs and connected with his crotch. Cole instinctively tried to grab at his now destroyed testicles, but his broken arms wouldn't allow it. Lisa took advantage of that and slammed the elbow part of the pipe directly down onto Cole's face. Then she dropped the pipe and spit into Cole's eye...again.

Josh was losing blood fast. He said, "We got to get you out of here. Go on up the stairs and out the back door. The cops will be here any minute."

Lisa said, "I'm not leaving you."

Josh shouted, "GO, I'll be right behind you. Find Wilkenson."

Lisa ran up the stairs and out into the cold night air. Josh grabbed his gloves that he had removed earlier and put them on his hands. Then he picked up the mirror with the coke on it. He walked over to Cole and looked down at him then dumped the remaining coke onto Cole's face and let the mirror drop. Josh said, "A little painkiller for you. You have got to be the dumbest motherfucker on the planet. Have fun being some big, burly prisoners bitch. They're gonna love you."

Josh could hear the sirens and slowly made his way up the stairs. He managed to get out the back door and fell down the outside steps and collapsed on the cold, hard ground. Snow had just begun to fall. The last thing he would remember seeing before passing out were the flashing blue and red lights reflecting on the old garage.

CHAPTER 17

Josh woke up suddenly shouting, "Lisa". He tried to sit up but the pain in his belly forced him back down onto the hospital bed.

He heard Aunt Lo's voice as she grabbed his shoulders trying to keep her nephew still "Josh, honey. Calm down."

"Lisa," Josh exclaimed. "Where's Lisa? Is she alright? I need to see her. Right now."

Lo said, "She's alright. She's safe."

"Where is she?"

"She's home." Lo said, "I sent her home to get some rest. She's hardly left your side since they brought you here."

"Where's here?" Josh said.

Lo said, "You're in the hospital. The doctor says you're going to be okay. Try to calm down so you don't pull out your stiches."

Josh was trying to catch his breath. He looked around the room and said, "How long have I been here?"

"Four days. You've been under sedation." Lo said, "You have a lot of pain meds in you. You've been asleep for a long time. Listen, Josh, you got shot. The doctors operated on you, but they said you're going to be alright. Please try to calm down."

Lo picked up the phone next to Josh's bed and tapped a number in it. "He's awake," She said into the phone.

"I need to see Lisa," Josh said.

Lo said, "I'll call her right now." She picked up the phone and waited for someone to answer. Finally, Josh heard her say, "It's Lo. He's awake and he's asking for you."

She listened for a moment then hung up the phone. "She's on her way."

She looked down at Josh and saw a single tear drop roll down his face near his ear. She said, "Josh, honey, what is it?"

Josh looked up at the ceiling and said, "It's all my fault."

"What?" Lo said. "What's all your fault?"

Josh said, "All of it. Lisa got hurt because of me. Because of what I did to those assholes"

"Stop that right now, Josh. None of this is your fault." Lo proclaimed.

"Of course it is" he said. "If I hadn't got Witch Hazel fired and not made a fool out of Jensen, none of this would have ever happened. She's going to hate me for this."

Lo said, "Oh Honey. Lisa will never hate you. You're her hero. You saved her life. You rescued her."

"There shouldn't have been a need to rescue her to begin with. Don't you see? I started this whole damn thing. It's all my fault." Josh said.

Lo began to tear up. She hated seeing her nephew like this.

She turned Josh's face to her and looking directly into his eyes said. "I want you to stop this right now. I mean it. This is not your fault and Lisa knows that."

"I'm afraid I'm going to lose her, Aunt Lo. Nothing scares me more than that."

"You are not going to lose her. You'll see." Lo said.

Just then the door to Josh's room opened and a lady in a lab coat walked in. She said, "Joshua, I'm Doctor Stephanie Lange. How do you feel?"

He said, "My belly hurts and my mouth hurts."

The doctor said, "That's understandable. You had a bullet in you that we had to remove. I know you don't feel lucky right now, but the bullet missed your spine by only a couple of inches. If it had hit your spine, you would most likely be in a wheelchair for the rest of your life."

"So, what happens now?" Josh asked.

The doctor said, "You'll survive. We had to patch up a few holes in you, but you'll be okay. No solid foods for a while until you heal."

"I can't have any of Aunt Lo's fried chicken? That sucks."

Lo smiled and said, "Not for quite some time, Buddy."

"What else, Doc?" Josh asked.

The doctor said, "That's pretty much it. Your black eye will disappear in a few days and your mouth will heal. You're going to be here for quite a while. We're going to continue with the IV for at least a couple of days and we're giving you antibiotics to prevent any infection. Remember, no solid foods. Clear liquids only until your belly heals up and keep still."

Doctor Lange left the room and Lo looked down at her

handsome nephew. She said, "You scared the hell out of me, Josh. You promised me you would never to do that again."

"I know," Josh said, "I'm sorry."

Lo said with a smile, "I'm going to let it go this time, but if you ever do it again, I'm cutting you off from my fried chicken for a year."

"I understand." Josh said, "Where are my clothes?"

Lo walked to a small closet and said, "In here."

Josh said, "Inside my right jeans pocket."

Lo reached in and pulled out Angel's necklace. Josh said, "Lisa needs that back."

The door to Josh's room opened a little while later and Lisa walked in. She smiled at Josh and said, "I'm glad you're awake, hero. I just talked to Lo in the hallway. She told me what you said."

Josh closed his eyes trying to fight back a tear. He said, "It's my fault, Lisa. There's no getting around that."

Lisa got close to Josh's face, grabbed his hand and spoke. "You listen to me. This was not your fault. You are not to blame yourself for any of it. I will never leave you. Understand? I love you more and more every day. You're my hero and you always will be. I was the one who dated that prick, remember?"

The lone tear streamed down Josh's cheek.

Lisa said, "Now you just have to get well and come home."

Josh nodded his head. He said, "I want to ask you something."

Lisa said, "What?"

He said, "Will you marry me?"

Lisa smiled and with no hesitation said, "It's about time you asked me. Yes, my hero, I will marry you."

Josh smiled and Lisa wrapped her arms around him as much as she could.

He said, "I have something for you." He opened his hand and Lisa looked down and saw the necklace he had given her. He said, "The clasp is broken, so I'll need to get it fixed for you."

* * *

Josh woke up the next morning and saw Lisa asleep in the chair next to his bed. He looked down and she was still holding his hand just like she was last night before he went to sleep. He tried to move but the pain in his belly kept messing with him. Lisa felt him stirring around and woke up. She said, "Babe, you need to stay still."

Josh said, "I have to move around some. I'm stiff and I'm getting sore laying here."

Lisa grabbed the controls for the bed and pressed a button, the head of the bed began to rise. She kept pressing the button until Josh was sitting almost all the way up. Then she pressed another button and Josh's knees started to bend. "Is that better?" she asked.

"Much better. Thank you, Babe" He said, "You'll make some lucky guy a great wife someday."

Lisa laughed and said, "Damn right I will and I'm certain I already found him."

Josh said, "Oh, yeah? What's he like?"

Lisa thought for a moment with a smile on her face, then she said, "Well, He's funny, smart, handsome. He takes real good care of me, he protects me and takes me on motorcycle rides with him." Then she whispered in his ear. "And he's really good in bed too."

Josh said, "Sounds like someone I know. He's a lucky, lucky man."

"Yes, he is," Lisa exclaimed. "Yes...he...is."

* * *

Lo tapped on the door and eased her way into Josh's room. She said, "You two aren't making out in here, are you?"

Lisa said, "I wish but his lips are still swollen and so are mine."

Lo said, "How ya feeling, Buddy?"

Josh said, "Great. I'm ready to go home."

Lo laughed and said, "Not yet"

Josh looked at her and said, "Where's my bacon and egg breakfast?

Lo shook her head and said, "Waiting for you at the house when you get out of here."

Josh said, "I do have some good news. I proposed to Lisa last night and she accepted."

Lo smiled and said, "Well it's about time."

Lisa laughed and looked at Josh who was busy rolling his eyes.

Lo said, "Congratulations. When's the date?"

Josh said, "I have a date in mind, but I haven't suggested it to her yet."

Lisa said, "You already have a date picked out? When?"

"September 7th," Josh said.

"Why September 7th?" Lisa asked.

Josh said, "Think about it, and if you can't guess why by that day, I'll explain it to you."

Lisa said, "Okay. Whatever you want, my hero."

Josh said, "I also have a location."

Lisa said, "The lake? First kiss?"

Josh smiled and said, "Is there any better place?"

"Absolutely not," Lisa said happily.

* * *

Later that morning there was another knock on the door. Lisa said, "Come in" and her family walked in, Dan, Nancy and Lori.

Dan said, "Josh, son. How ya feeling?"

Josh said, "I'm ready to go home and get Uncle Woody's bike out."

They all chuckled because they knew that wasn't going to happen for a long time.

They visited for a while but couldn't stay long. Dan had a business to run, and Lori was busy with school stuff. Nancy said, "We're so happy you two are okay."

The family got ready to leave and Josh asked if Dan could stay for a few minutes. He had something to discuss with him. They all looked at him with puzzled looks on their faces except Lisa who was smiling. Nancy, Lisa, Lo and Lori all walked out into the hallway.

Josh said to Dan, "Sir, I'm sorry I put Lisa in a dangerous position. I promise it'll never happen again."

Dan said, "Son, you have nothing to apologize for. You rescued our daughter again. We are all thankful for you."

Josh hesitated for a second and said, "Sir, you know how much I care for your daughter. I've asked her to marry me, and she accepted. I would like to have your blessing."

Dan smiled and said, "Well, it's about time."

Josh said, "Why does everyone keep saying that? Aunt Lo and Lisa both said the same thing."

Dan chuckled and said, "I'd be honored to be your father-in-law, son, under one condition."

"What's that?"

Dan said, "Only if you agree to stop calling me, 'sir' and call me Dan instead."

Josh said, "Okay, Dan…sir."

Dan smiled and said, "You take care of yourself and my daughter. We'll see you soon."

Dan walked out of the room. A few seconds later Josh heard Lori's voice out in the hallway say loudly, "IT'S ABOUT TIME."

* * *

Officer Scott Wilkenson walked into Josh's room. So many visitors had come by that Lisa decided to just leave the door open.

Officer Wilkenson said, "Mr. Bailey. How ya doin'?"

Josh said, "About as good as I look."

The officer said, "That bad, huh?"

That made Josh, Lo and Lisa smile.

Josh said, "What's the good word?"

"Well," the officer said, "They've both been charged with a variety of crimes. Cole Jensen has been charged with kidnapping, assault, assault with a deadly weapon, attempted murder and attempted rape. Sam Blackwell has been charged with kidnapping, theft and assault. There may be more charges filed later. Both are in a hospital in Wichita. For their own safety."

Josh looked over at Lisa who had a slight smile on her face.

Josh said, "So they're alive?"

"By some miracle. You really did a number on them. Neither of them will probably ever walk the same again." Officer Wilkenson said.

"You know I could have easily killed both of them."

Officer Wilkenson said, "We know. We got Lisa's statement that night and when you're ready, I need your statement as well."

Josh asked, "Can you give me a day or so?"

"Sure," the officer said, "You know, the bad guys in this town had a good thing going for them until you got here."

Josh quipped with a smile, "Always ready to do your job for you."

"Right", Officer Wilkenson said, "I'll check on you in a day or so. Feel better, Josh. You did real good."

* * *

That afternoon, Lance and Becky strolled into the room. Lance said, "Where's this hero…." He stopped when he saw his buddy. "Dude, you look like shit."

Becky backhanded Lance in the chest and said, "Lance. That's not nice."

"He knows I'm just messing with him," Lance said,

Josh said, "Don't make me laugh, it hurts."

Lance said, "But that's my job. My function."

Becky said, "Not at the moment, it isn't." She looked at Josh and said, "How are feeling, Mr. Hero?"

"Ready to go home," Josh said.

Lisa said, "That's been his go-to response all day."

Josh said, "How you doing, Beck? Is this clown treating you alright?"

Becky smiled and said, "Yeah. Most of the time. We were worried about you."

"I'll be fine."

Lance said, "You know, at some point you have to stop being the hero and let someone else save you for a change."

Josh looked at Lisa and said to everyone, "I have my hero. She's sitting right there." He continued, "and she's going to marry me in September."

Lance and Becky's faces lit up. "It's about time," they both said simultaneously.

"What the hell?" Josh said.

Lisa was laughing hard, she said, "Everyone says that when we tell them. Even my dad."

Lance and Becky stayed for about a half hour. Lisa told them the story of what happened. They asked questions and Lisa and Josh would answer them. When it came time for them to go, Lance grabbed Josh's hand and said, "I'm glad you're okay. Get well so we can go do something."

Becky walked to Josh and bent down to hug him. She said, "We love you, Josh. You're everyone's hero."

As they got close to the door, Becky turned around and said, "Lance was right, though. You do look like shit." She smiled, winked at Josh and walked out the door behind Lance. Lisa walked out with them leaving Lo and Josh alone.

Lo said, "Are you okay?"

"Just a lot of excitement. There are lot of visitors. Too much attention."

Lo said, "Do you think you can handle a few more?"

Josh said, "I don't know. I'm tired. All this attention."

Lo said, "Try to hang on for just a few more minutes then we'll let you get some rest."

Just then Lisa walked back into the room. Lo asked her, "Is everything all set?"

Lisa nodded and said, "Ready to go."

Lo stood up and said, "We have something to show you, Josh." She opened the blinds of the window and Josh looked outside his first-floor room. Standing outside were at least 50 or more people all looking at Josh. They were all smiling and waving. Some had signs that said, 'Get well soon' or 'Josh, you're our hero'. Josh was surprised. He wasn't expecting anything quite like that. He raised his hand and waved to all of them. They were cheering and chanting. "We love you, Josh" some yelled. "Get well soon" and "You're our hero"

Josh said to Lisa, "Is it safe to assume that your dad had something to do with this?"

"Can't put anything past you," Lisa said

Josh looked sad and Lisa noticed. Lisa said, "I think he's had enough excitement for one day."

Lo looked at her nephew, saw the look on his face and said, "I agree" she waved at the well-wishers and closed the blinds.

They both looked at Josh and he said, "I wish everyone would stop calling me a hero. It's fine if it's you two but it makes me uncomfortable when other people do it."

Lo and Lisa looked at each other and nodded. Lisa said, "But you are a hero. You're MY hero and Lo's too"

Josh said to Lisa, "Remember back in seventh grade when Witch Hazel got fired? Everyone at school kept calling me a 'hero'. I didn't like it then and I don't like it now. You and Aunt Lo are the only ones that I want to be a hero to. I love it when YOU call me your hero and when Aunt Lo calls me your hero but not everyone else. It's difficult to explain why."

Lo said, "I think we both understand."

The next day around mid-morning a gentleman, well-dressed in a suit and tie walked into Josh's room. He was good sized man with perfectly combed hair, and he was carrying a briefcase.

Lisa was sitting in what had become 'her chair' next to Josh.

The man announced himself as Brandon Hall. He said he was the prosecutor and would be trying Cole and Sam. He asked Lisa and Josh if he could speak with them. Josh and Lisa nodded.

Brandon Hall said, "First, I'm glad you two are okay. It must have been a horrible thing to experience. Especially for you, Ms. Fisher."

"Please, call me Lisa."

"Very well. I read the statement you gave to the police. I understand that you'll be giving them your statement soon as well, Mr. Bailey?"

"Josh or Joshua," Josh said. "Probably this afternoon."

"Good." Mr. Hall said.

Josh asked. "What are we looking at as far as punishment goes for those two?"

"If it goes to trial, that is to say, if they don't plead guilty, then we're going for the max for both of them." The Prosecutor said, "They're looking at 30 years for Jensen and 20 years for Blackwell"

Josh looked at Lisa, he said, "Does that sound fair to you, Babe?"

Lisa said, "No."

Josh said, "There you go."

The prosecutor said, "Here's the thing. Cole Jensen has only one arrest for DUI and Sam Blackwell has no record."

Josh said, "I think I can speak for both of us when I say, 'we don't care'". Josh glanced at Lisa who was nodding her head. Josh continued, "Jensen assaulted Lisa and if I hadn't come along when I did, that sonofabitch would've raped her. Blackwell abducted her and assaulted her. I'm going to tell you right now that I've had experience dealing with courts when I was a kid. I have very little faith in them. Scratch that. I have ZERO faith in them."

"I understand your frustration," Hall said.

"No, you don't" Josh was getting angry, and Lisa could tell but she wasn't about to stop him. "Did you watch your mother die at the hands of someone who had been released from jail many times? I highly doubt it. I allowed those two assholes to live because I wanted to give the law and the courts one more chance to do the right thing. They could be dead right now and I would be justified in doing it. But I didn't kill them. Don't make me regret that."

The prosecutor thought for a moment. Josh looked at Lisa and she nodded at Josh.

The prosecutor said, "I'll do my best."

Josh said, "Uh-huh." He looked at Lisa and said, "Babe, what do you think?"

Lisa said plainly and flatly. "50 years for Jensen and 35 years for Blackwell."

Josh nodded in agreement and said to the prosecutor. "There you have it. That's the justice she wants and that's the justice she should receive."

The prosecutor stood and got ready to leave. He spoke. "All I can say is I'll do my best."

Lisa said, "No plea deals until you talk to us. I promise you that with the good people of this community and our standing in it, you'll never be re-elected. I can guarantee that. Don't even think about taking a deal without our approval."

The prosecutor picked up his briefcase and walked out.

* * *

Later in the day Officer Wilkinson got Josh's statement. It wasn't any different than what Lisa had told him a few days before except Lisa had more to tell him since she was the one who was abducted. The Officer thanked them and went about his day.

* * *

Not long after the officer left, Lo walked in then stopped and poked her head back out the door opening and waved someone in. Seconds later, in walked Emily and Jessica. Josh perked right up when he saw them. He shouted, "Em. Look at you walking around with crutches."

"Hey, little brother. How ya doing?" Emily asked.

"Much better now," Josh said with a grin. "It looks like we've reversed roles."

"Yes, it does, doesn't it."

Lisa rose from her chair and went to hug the two girls. "It's so good to see you." She said.

"Hey, Jess," Josh said. "Sit down, both of you."

He asked how they were doing and what's been going on. Emily said that she was pretty much healed. Thanks to her doctor.

Josh smiled and said, "You mean the Doc I think you should marry?"

Jessica laughed and Emily looked at her rolling her eyes. Emily said to Jessica, "Go ahead and tell him. I know you're dying to."

Jessica said, "They're dating."

Josh laughed and said, "That's terrific." He laughed some more.

Emily was blushing and Josh pointed it out to everyone.

They all shared a laugh at Emily's expense. It was all in jest. They were happy for her. Then Josh said, "Now we just need to find a guy for you, Jess."

Now it was Emily's turn to laugh. Josh said, "I have someone in mind for you too."

Lisa looked at Josh and said, "Who?"

Josh smiled and said, "Wilkenson."

Lisa smiled and said, "He's perfect for her."

"I know, right?"

Emily smiled at Jessica then looked back at Josh and said, "Who's that?"

"He's a cop here in town. He's a great guy" he turned to look at Jess and said, "You'd like him. I'll introduce you to him sometime.

Lo said, "Lisa, let's go to the cafeteria and get something to drink so these three can catch up."

Lisa and Lo left and closed the door behind them.

Emily said, "I want to thank you again for what you did. The whole city was shocked and pleased to have that monster off the streets. You really do hate bullies, don't you?"

Josh smiled and said, "I don't know what you're talking about." Then winked at her.

They both smiled back at him. They got it.

* * *

Two weeks later, Doctor Stephanie entered josh's room and said, "Are you ready to go home?"

Josh said, "I was ready to go home when I got here."

* * *

One month after Josh was released from the hospital, He, Lisa and Aunt Lo were in the front room at Lo's house talking to Brandon Hall. Mr. Hall said, "They're willing to plead guilty on all counts. 45 years for Jensen and 30 years for Blackwell. That's only five years each less than what you asked for. If we go to court, it's unlikely they would get much over that. Plus, going to court, each of you would have to testify and the trial would take place at least three months from now."

Josh looked at Lisa who was busy doing the math in her head. Finally, she said, "Cole will be sixty-six when he gets out and Sam will be fifty-one." She looked at Josh and he shrugged.

He said, "It's your call."

Lisa said, "I don't want to deal with a trial and plan a wedding at the same time." She looked at the prosecutor and said, "Take the deal."

CHAPTER 18

Two months before the wedding, Lisa and Josh found the perfect home for sale. It was yellow with white shutters, one story (not counting the basement), 3 bedrooms and 2 ½ baths and a two-car garage. Better yet, it was located halfway between Lisa's parent's home and Lo's home. Perfect. Lisa told the realtor, "We'll take it." Then she turned to Josh and said, "We're going to make many wonderful memories here."

Josh said, "Yes, we are."

The wedding plans were going well. Aunt Lo and her good friend, Nancy worked well as a team and wedding coordinators. They both had the same tastes and ideas. Lisa and Josh had asked them to keep it simple and to keep costs down, which Lisa's father, Dan, appreciated very much. Lo and Josh had offered to pay for half, but Dan would have none of that. Lisa chose sky blue to be her color as it was both Her's and Josh's favorite color. The wedding would be held at the lake where Josh and Lisa had their first kiss. The ceremony would be on the shore with the lake as a backdrop. The shelter house less than 50 feet from the shore would be used for their reception. It would be catered for by a local restaurant owner who insisted on giving Dan a discount since Dan had helped him in the past.

* * *

Thursday, September 6th.
The day before the wedding.

For months people asked, "Why September 7th? That's a Friday. Why not have it on a Saturday?"

Lisa would always respond, "That's the date Josh chose. I don't know why he chose it, but I agreed to it. I know he must have a reason."

Lance, Becky, Josh, and Lisa were at Pizza Hut having another good time reminiscing and talking about tomorrow's big day. Lance would be Josh's best man and of course, Becky would be Lisa's maid of honor. It was Josh and Lisa's last night as boyfriend and girlfriend. In twenty-four hours, they would be husband and wife. Neither of them could stop smiling and having their best friends with them made that task even more difficult.

After they had finished eating, Becky said, "Okay, Josh. Fess up. It's time to tell us why you chose September 7th."

That perked Lisa up because she knew Josh wouldn't lead Becky on or lie to her. He would tell all. She had been waiting for months to find out the answer. She simply trusted Josh to tell her when the time was right.

Josh smiled, looked at Lisa and he said, "When I first got here, you were the first person I met, other than Gus my bus driver. I was waiting in Witch Hazels' office, and she called out for you to show me around the school."

Lisa said, "I remember that."

Josh said, "It was September 7th, 1982. Eight years ago, tomorrow."

Everyone at the table laughed with joy. Lisa said, "Oh my god. You remember the date?"

Josh said, "Of course I do. It was the most important day of my life. Tomorrow it will become the second most important day of my life."

Lisa grinned and said, "I can't wait to tell my dad. He's been bugging me about it for months. He's going to love this."

Josh said, "Your turn. Who's officiating?

Since Josh left Lisa hanging as to why he chose the date. Lisa kept the secret of who would be officiating the wedding for months.

Lisa said, "You're going to love this. I called Pastor Stevens in Pleasanton, and he happily agreed to do it for us."

Josh was thrilled to hear this. He said, "You couldn't have made a better choice. You are amazing."

Lisa said, "I know."

September 7th, 1990.
Wedding day!

It was going to be a beautiful fall day. The sun was shining, and the temperature would be in the upper 60s.

Loanne had risen early and made breakfast for Josh and Lance. Becky was with Lisa. Lance said, "Best bacon and eggs I've ever had. What's your secret?"

Lo said, "I'm not telling."

There was much to do for Aunt Lo. She had to meet Nancy at the lake and finish decorating the shelter house. Then come home and change clothes before going back to the lake for the wedding which was scheduled for 5:00 p.m. They had decided that time so Lori wouldn't miss a day of school. She would miss basketball practice but that was fine.

Josh would ride Woody's Harley out to the lake and Lance would follow him and bring him back so he could change later. Josh and Lisa would ride off into the sunset on Woody's Harley after the wedding.

Dan had found a nice camper trailer he could borrow that Lisa could use at the lake to prepare for her big day. She and Becky would be there all day. Aunt Lo took some jeans and a t-shirt for Josh and left them in the trailer so Josh would have something to wear when they departed on Woody's bike.

* * *

At 4:00, Lance and Josh arrived at the lake. Lo took one look at Josh and said, "There's my handsome nephew."

Josh was dressed in the same suit he had worn for Uncle Woody's funeral. Only now he had a sky-blue tie and a blue boutonniere.

Josh looked around and saw all the hard work Nancy and

Aunt Lo had put into decorating the shelter house. They did a fantastic job. Down at the shore, there were a few rows of chairs facing the lake. There wouldn't be enough seating for everyone but the ceremony itself wouldn't take long and most folks were happy to stand.

As time went on, guests began arriving and milling about in the open shelter house. Officer Scott Wilkenson was there and many of the area farmers and storekeepers were there as well. Pastor Stevens arrived, and Josh thanked him profusely for officiating. Pastor Stevens said, "It's my honor." Dan was busying himself with greeting everyone. He was making sure that everyone felt welcome. Shaking hands with all the guests. Josh had an uneasy feeling about something but couldn't figure out what it was.

Josh was standing alone several feet away from the shelter house when Aunt Lo walked up to him. She said, "Are you okay?"

Josh nodded and said, "Look at all these people, Aunt Lo. They're all smiling and dressed up so nice."

Aunt Lo said, "They have a lot to smile about. It's an important day."

Josh stood silent for a moment then he said, "I miss him. I wish he were here. He would love this."

Lo smiled and said, "He is here."

Josh looked at her with a puzzled look.

She said, "Here's what I do. I imagine that he is here. Walking around. Talking to people. Smiling." She looked right into Josh's eyes and said, "If you believe he's here, then he will be. In your heart and mind. It doesn't mean it has to be true physically, you just have to believe it. That's all."

That made him feel better. Then Lo said, "Look who's coming." And walked away to greet someone.

Josh looked up at the sky, tapped his heart with his fist, and pointed up to the sky smiling.

Then he heard his name being shouted. "Joshua Bailey!"

He turned around and saw his sister, Emily, walking toward him. With her was her doctor and Jessica. They hugged and Emily re-introduced her boyfriend to Josh. She said, "Josh this is…"

Josh cut her off and said, "Doctor Hinson. It's a pleasure to see you again"

They shook hands and the doctor said, "Congratulations on your wedding."

Josh said, "Thank you. Thank you for coming." He smiled at his sister, winked at her, and whispered in her ear, "I told you."

Then he hugged Jessica and said, "There's someone here I want you to meet."

"Oh, shit," Jessica responded.

Josh said, "See that guy over there with the bald head talking to that other guy?"

Jessica said warily, "Yeah."

"That's Officer Scott Wilkenson."

"He's bald," Jessica exclaimed.

Josh winked at Emily and said, "Not the bald guy, that's Lisa's dad. I'm talking about the one he's talking to."

Jessica focused her eyes on Wilkenson and said, "He's cute."

Josh said, "You want to meet him?"

Jessica said, "Why not?"

"Come on," Josh said and escorted Jessica over to meet Officer Scott Wilkenson.

* * *

Pastor Stevens took his place near the shore of the lake and announced they would begin soon and would like everyone to take their seats. Josh and Lance were standing off to the side, Lance shook Josh's hand and said, "I knew this day would come back in the seventh grade."

Josh said, "Don't make me laugh right now, dickhead."

Lance chuckled, patted Josh on his shoulder, and said, "Let's get you hitched."

They took their places and watched as Lo walked down the aisle, smiling grandly, and took her seat.

Then Nancy and Lori walked down and took her seats on the left side. They didn't use ushers. Then Becky strolled her way down the aisle with an angry look on her face. As she approached Josh she suddenly grinned and winked at him and Lance.

The Wedding March began to play from speakers in the shelter house. The door to the camper opened and Dan was standing and waiting for his daughter. He held out his hand and she grabbed it as she carefully made her way down the steps. She looked absolutely stunning. Her white dress had small blue flowers around the top and she was showing just enough cleavage to give Josh a tease. Her train was very short. Only going down to the base of her back. Josh would learn later that she designed it that way because he was so fond of her perfect ass (according to

Becky). The hem of her white skirt rested halfway up her thighs (another tease).

Those who were seated rose to their feet as Dan escorted his daughter down the aisle. Josh couldn't stop grinning as he watched his bride walk down the aisle. Lisa had the same problem.

Dan placed his daughter's hand in Josh's hand, kissed his daughter on the cheek, shook Josh's hand, and said to him, "Take good care of my daughter."

Josh smiled and said, "I will...sir."

Dan turned, smiling, shaking his head, and sat down next to his wife, Nancy.

Pastor Stevens looked out at everyone and said, "We have gathered here today to join Joshua Bailey and Lisa Fisher in holy matrimony"

Suddenly everyone attending shouted, "IT'S ABOUT TIME." And laughed uproariously.

Josh turned to look at Dan. Dan pointed his finger at Josh and said, "Got ya."

Pastor Stevens recited some scripture from the Bible and then had them recite their vows. Then he said, "Do you have the rings?"

Lisa turned slightly and Becky placed Josh's band in Lisa's hand. Josh turned to Lance with his hand open. Lance looked at Josh and said, "What?"

Josh said, "The ring."

Lance said, "What ring?"

Becky heard him and said, "Lance! Not now."

Lance smiled, dug into his pocket pulled out Lisa's ring, and handed it to Josh.

Everyone chuckled. Even Dan.

When they were all done, Pastor Stevens said, "You may kiss the bride." Josh and Lisa were more than happy to oblige him. Everyone cheered and applauded. Then Pastor Stevens said, "It is my privilege and honor to introduce to you as husband and wife. "Mr. and Mrs. Joshua Bailey."

Josh and Lisa were mobbed with well-wishers congratulating them and hugging them.

Aunt Lo stood aside, looked up at the sky, and said, "We did it." And smiled.

When she was finally able to get to her nephew she said, "Woody would be so proud of you."

Josh said, "I know he is."

While the guests were enjoying their meal, the wedding party was down on the shore getting photos taken by a photographer Lisa had chosen. The lake with the trees on the other side made a perfect backdrop. When it came time for just the Bride and Groom to get their pictures alone, Josh and Lisa stood while the photographer snapped several photos. When she was done, Josh looked at Lisa and they smiled at each other and kissed. While they were kissing, they heard a loud chirping sound in a nearby tree. They both turned to look and on one of the lower branches sat a bluejay chirping happily. They looked at each other, chuckled then looked back at the beautiful blue bird smiling. Lisa said, "I think she approves."

Josh said, "I believe you're right."

Then the bluejay flew away.

* * *

Once everyone had finished their meals and had all offered their congratulations to Josh and Lisa. The newlyweds made their way to the camper to change. Lance being Lance shouted, "If this camper's rocking, don't bother knocking." Becky backhanded him in his chest...again.

Inside the camper, after Lisa and Josh were fully dressed, Lisa took Josh into her arms and said, "I have something to tell you. I'm pregnant."

Josh was elated. He hugged his new bride tightly and said, "That's the best thing I've heard since you said, 'I do.'"

* * *

Several minutes later, Lisa and Josh exited the camper. Both were in their riding clothes.

Josh is in his jeans, boots, and a black T-shirt. Lisa was in her jeans with a tight, black Harley shirt and boots. Everyone waiting outside the camper tossed birdseed over the couple as they made their way to Woody's Harley.

Just as he was about to climb on the bike, Josh noticed Aunt Lo who was standing near Emily, smiling. He ran to his sister and hugged her then stepped to Aunt Lo, hugged her tightly, and said, "Thank you so much for rescuing me."

With a happy tear streaming down her beautiful face, Aunt Lo said, "Thank you for being such a wonderful nephew to me and Woody." She kissed him on the cheek and said, "Now get out of here." Smiling proudly.

Josh whispered in his Aunt Lo's ear, "She's pregnant." Then raced back to Woody's bike.

Josh brought his leg over the bike and Lisa, as Josh had instructed her to do on their second date and had done many times since, climbed on behind him. Josh fired up the Harley and worked the throttle a couple of times then said, "Are you ready, my lady?"

Lisa said, "Let 'er rip."

Josh slowly released the clutch lever and as they pulled away Lisa wrapped her arms around Josh's chest and shouted over the loud pipes so everyone could hear. "I love you, my Hero!" Josh smiled, reached down, and with his left hand gave his bride a love tap on her calf.

EPILOGUE

Almost nine months to the day after their wedding. Lisa and Josh welcomed their daughter, Angel Loanne Bailey, into the world. Lisa insisted on the name, she said, "When we have another daughter, we'll name her Emily Nancy." Baby Angel had blonde hair and smiled a lot. Two years later, they would welcome their son, Woodrow Daniel Bailey into the world as well. Little Woody had red hair and was a strapping baby. Lisa said, "He's going to be a heartbreaker someday."

Great-grand Aunt Lo and Grandma Nancy would spoil the children to no end. Grandpa Dan enjoyed reading to his grandchildren.

During this time, Emily married her doctor. Lance and Becky got married at the same location as Josh and Lisa. You can guess who the matron-of-honor and the best man were. Officer Scott Wilkenson left Anthony and joined the police force in St. Joseph.

Joshua Bailey swore to himself that he would never take a human life again.

Made in the USA
Columbia, SC
28 November 2024

47134776R00152